killing britney

killing britney

SEAN OLIN

SIMON PULSE
New York   London   Toronto   Sydney

This book is a work of fiction. Any references to historical events, real people, or real locales are used fictitiously. Other names, characters, places, and incidents are the product of the author's imagination, and any resemblance to actual events or locales or persons, living or dead, is entirely coincidental.

First Simon Pulse edition July 2005

SIMON PULSE
An imprint of Simon & Schuster Children's Publishing Division
1230 Avenue of the Americas, New York, NY 10020

 Produced by Alloy Entertainment
151 West 26th Street
New York, NY 10001

Printed in the United States of America
10 9 8 7 6 5 4 3 2 1

Library of Congress Control Number 2004115721
ISBN 0-689-87778-1

killing britney

one

The La Follette Rabid Raccoons were slaughtering the Sun Prairie Prairie Dogs by a score of five to one, and Britney Johnson was riveted as always. She was sitting with her new friends, all of whom, like her, dated hockey players. They called themselves the hockey wives and they had their own special section of Madison Arena: front row center, right behind the thick Plexiglas.

The Raccoons were the best high school hockey team in Wisconsin, and Britney's boyfriend, Ricky Piekowski, was a starting defenseman. He didn't score a lot, but he was a real threat to the opposition. Today, in the second quarter, he'd checked the Prairie Dogs' star, Todd Smaltz, right in front of her. Smaltz had been breaking away, flicking the puck back and forth up the ice, and he hadn't seen Ricky coming up behind him. Just as Smaltz was about to cross the blue line, Ricky thrust his shoulder into Smaltz's back, skated through him, and pile-drove his head into the glass.

It all happened so close to Britney that she could hear Ricky's grunt. She could hear Smaltz's whimper. The glass rattled and bent and she'd thought for a second that it would shatter, spraying shards down onto her and her friends. Instead, Todd Smaltz shattered; he crumpled to the ice and lay there, barely moving, just twitching his right foot a little. He had to be carried off on a stretcher and taken to the hospital.

As punishment for this, Ricky was given five minutes in the penalty box.

Britney frowned. "Hey, Erin, isn't that legal?" she asked.

Erin screwed up her nose and rolled her eyes as she shook her head like a bobble-head doll. "Of course it's legal," she said. "The refs are all against us. They'll give us penalties for anything. If they could, they'd put the whole team in the penalty box and let the other team shoot up the score against an empty field."

Britney grinned. "It wouldn't help. Once our guys got out, they'd get it all back. There'd be hat tricks for everyone." She hoped what she'd said made sense.

She didn't really know much about the rules of hockey. Most of what she knew she'd learned in the past six months. She understood the basics—that to get a point, you needed to flick the puck into the net. She had a vague understanding that the blue line was somehow important. But whenever she tried to actually follow the action, she ended up spending the whole game confused. The puck zoomed all over the place, moving so quickly that half the time she couldn't find it. The trick of following what was going on was to watch the players—*they* seemed to always know where the puck was—as they sped back and forth in their crimson headgear and oversized uniforms.

Still, watching the guys play was always exciting. What she responded to was the atmosphere of controlled chaos. Ricky and his buddies shaking things up, knocking heads, and beating the opposition into submission. All in the name of winning.

She loved being one of the select group of girls who got to be with the team: when the guys won, she felt like she had won as well. She loved cheering them on.

Ricky's penalty had squelched the excitement in the crowd, so Erin called the wives into a huddle and clapped sharply three times in a row. The hockey team didn't have cheerleaders, so the hockey wives had to get the crowd going themselves. Erin was the ringmaster. As she scanned the faces lined up around her— Cindy and Daphney and Jodi and Britney—she cocked the side of her mouth and narrowed her eyes.

"Listen up, folks, this crowd is way, way too quiet."

As she spoke, she looked back and forth down the row, and her blond ponytail flicked across her shoulders.

"Let's do 'Iron,' cool?"

The five of them jumped up from their bench and turned to face the stands above them.

"One," shouted Erin. The other girls joined in. "Two. Three."

"Hard as iron

Strong as steel

Rabid Raccoons

How you feel?"

And the fans in the stands around them roared.

Britney loved the power rush of leading the crowd like this. She loved being the center of attention. She loved knowing that everyone was watching her.

Even though Madison Arena was chilly, she was careful about how she dressed for games, wearing her tightest, lowest-riding blue jeans and a yellow spaghetti strap tank top that showed off the two wings she'd gotten tattooed across the small of her back last summer. Probably the other people in the stands saw the wings as mere adornments meant to call attention to her sexy butt, but to Britney they meant much, much more than that. They were swan's wings. And they symbolized how far she'd come from being the dorky, depressed little nerd she once was.

She'd always loved swans. When she was six, her father had read her "The Ugly Duckling" and it had stuck with her, popping into her mind fairly frequently throughout the lonely years of middle school and high school. She'd identified with the little bird, mocked and laughed at for being unusual until it grew up to be especially gifted and beautiful. Finally, last year, she'd decided that if she was going to sparkle and bloom into her glory, maybe she should work at it a little bit. She'd dyed her mousy brown hair blond, but not too blond, subtly high-lighted so that it looked almost like her natural color when it was streaked by the summer sun. She worked out and did the Atkins diet to keep off the baby fat, and the result was a flat stomach and toned thighs but also slightly smaller boobs than she'd like—she fixed that, though, with a Wonder Bra.

Throughout the final two minutes of the game, Ricky and his buddies—they called themselves the Unstoppables and hadn't lost a game since they played Appleton in the state championship two years ago—began to taunt the Prairie Dogs. Instead of trying to score, they played keep-away. They started toying with the puck, shooting it back and forth to one another, pushing it right up under the Prairie Dogs' noses and then yanking it back again.

"See," said Erin, leaning in toward Britney, "this is how they get themselves in trouble. Ricky's already made the Dogs mad, and now they're just making it worse."

Daphney popped her head in too. She was tall and had a long, elegant neck. "Well, what do you expect from them? That's what they *do*. Remember when Digger and Jeremy got in that fight with the guy in the parking lot after the Racine game last year?"

"That was insane," said Erin. "That guy must have been crazy to think they'd let him call them out like that without a fight."

Whenever they talked about events from before she began dating Ricky, Britney felt left out. "When was that?" she asked.

"What happened?" But Erin and Daphney were absorbed in each other now, reminiscing over things that were before her time.

"Remember how the guy's girlfriend kept trying to pull him away?" said Jodi, taking a long pull on the straw jabbed into her Mountain Dew.

Daphney laughed. "She and some other girl got in front of him and he tried to spit at Digger, like, to launch a fat lugie—"

Erin couldn't hold herself back. She finished Daphney's sentence for her. "And it flew back in the wind and hit his girlfriend on the back of the head."

They all giggled at this. All except Britney, who had shrunk a little in her place on the bench, waiting for them to return to a topic that was familiar to her.

Cindy, the most beautiful of the wives, with her black ringlets and piercing blue eyes, leaned over toward her. "You should watch out for those hockey wives too, Britney. They can be vicious."

Britney arched an eyebrow. "Whatever," she said. "Ricky would kill them." It was inconceivable that she might actually be in danger, but all this passion swirling around in the air was exciting.

When the game was over, the girls struggled to push through the crowd toward the tunnel that led to the locker rooms. This was where everyone congregated at the conclusion of every game, and getting past the throngs was tough to do, even for people as obviously important as the hockey wives.

The one thing about herself that Britney couldn't fix was how short she was. To locate Ricky among the mob of students and players celebrating in the tunnel right now, she had to jump up and down like a pogo stick and grab quick glances above the heads of the crowd.

When she finally found him, Ricky was all the way across the rink, surrounded by his crew, Troy, Digger, and Jeremy. They were doing their hand thing—high five, low five, gotcha-too-slow five, pound the fist, grab the wrist, slide and smoke the blunt—and, she was sure, going over every great play they'd made tonight and speculating about how badly Todd Smaltz was hurt. The rumor was that he'd broken his back.

Heading off in Ricky's direction, Britney squeezed and elbowed her way through the throngs of students, most of whom had painted their faces red and gold.

And then she stopped. She froze.

Standing alone amid the revelers, typically speaking to no one and acting like he was above it all with his arms folded tight over his chest, was Bobby Plumley. Unlike everyone else, his acne-ridden face wasn't painted. Underneath his greasy brown bowl cut, he was smirking at her, staring. Britney bugged her eyes and glared back at him, then pushed her way through a group of skinny freshman boys, their winter parkas zipped up to their chins, who were awkwardly stumbling all over each other, trying their best to look cool.

When she reached Ricky, she leapt into his arms and threw her own around his shoulders. He hadn't seen her coming, and he was startled at first, stumbling under her weight, but when he caught his balance, he grinned and kissed her.

"Hey, angel," he said.

She whispered into his ear, "You were great."

"I think I really messed that guy up."

"If he can't handle it, he shouldn't be playing."

Ricky frowned. His eyes wandered off to a worried place inside his head, and Britney wondered if it was a sign of regret or some other, more complicated emotion. "Smaltz had it coming to him anyway," Ricky said. "Last year he high-sticked Digger in the head so bad he had to get eight stitches above his eye."

She kissed him and then joined the other wives to wait in the tunnel for the guys to change out of their uniforms.

Then it was off to the kegger at Troy's place.

Troy lived in a large yellow split-level ranch house half a mile out of town. Across the street from his house was an abandoned dairy farm with an old red barn and two wooden silos. His parents were always away in Chicago on the weekends, and his parties were legendary.

Tonight was his first big blowout of the hockey season. Kid Rock was turned up so loud that the windows rattled in their frames. The furniture had been moved from the living room to make space for dancing. All the Raccoons were there. So were all the hockey wives. Everyone who was anyone in school had been invited: Travis Lawson, the school president and his crew of preppies, the guys from Hummus, the Phish cover band that was already so big they were playing University of Wisconsin frat houses. Art Richter, who sold pot around school, was camped out in Troy's bedroom with his stoner buddies—every time the door opened, smoke came wafting out as if they had lit the curtains on fire.

Before she started dating Ricky, Britney had never been to one of Troy's parties. Last year she hadn't been important enough to invite, and even if she had been invited, she would have felt too awkward and scared to go.

Even now that she was with Ricky, she often felt odd, like she didn't quite fit in. She constantly felt like she was faking it and that people would eventually discover she wasn't as cool as they thought she was. So, tonight, she shyly hung close to Ricky and his hockey player friends. They were shotgunning cans of Milwaukee's Best at the island counter in the kitchen, competing to see who could drink the most.

"Hey, Britney," Ricky said for the fifth time in twenty minutes. "You should try this. It's easy. You just open your throat. You won't gag, I promise."

"No, that's okay," she said again, smiling demurely and hoping her face wasn't turning red.

When Digger suggested that they all play quarters, Ricky said, "That's a great idea. I think Britney should start."

She glared at him and said no yet again, but the damage was done. Erin said, "Don't be a priss, Britney. It's just beer. It's not like we're trying to make you drink Drano or something." All the other hockey wives were lined up ready to play, watching to see if she'd finally bend.

"Maybe later," she said. She shook her head at Ricky, simmering inside, but there wasn't anything she could say at that moment, not in front of all these people.

She didn't drink. She didn't like ever to be out of control. And he knew this. It was hard not to get annoyed. She suspected he was just showing off for his friends, and the thought of this made her want to run away. But she knew he'd get upset if she wasn't there next to him, pretending to pay attention to their inane argument about which animal could beat which in a fight—lion or hyena, rattler or rhino, elephant or mouse.

When "Wish You Were Here," by Incubus started blasting out of the stereo speakers, everyone pounded their beer cans down on the counter and ran to the living room to slam dance. It was total chaos. Twelve massive hockey players, plus the whole wrestling team, squished into one not very large room, head butting and throwing shoulders at each other. Digger jumped onto Ricky's back and they started swinging each other around the room. The rest of the crowd pulled back to watch them brawl.

Britney used this distraction to make her escape. She went downstairs to the basement, where the big-screen TV was, and sat by herself, watching *The Matrix* with the sound off. The ceiling above her head vibrated as people upstairs jumped around to the music, but the noise was muffled and far away as if she had entered an eerie remote place where nothing, not even sound, could reach her.

Eventually Ricky found her down there. "What are you doing?" he said. "You're making me look bad! The guys are all saying they saw you run off with that hippie guy from Hummus!"

She couldn't believe it. He was mad at her! But he was the one who'd been being a jerk. It was all just so typical.

two

Britney and Ricky had begun fighting at Troy's party after he'd found her alone in the basement. Even though she was the only one down there, he'd accused her of flirting with other guys.

Now, nearly an hour later, idling the car in front of her father's big house in the Green Pastures housing development, Ricky still wouldn't let it go. His anger seemed to have more to do with the teasing he'd had to put up with from Jeremy and Digger than with anything that Britney herself had done. They'd used her absence as an excuse to pummel his shoulder and say things like, "You better watch out for her, man. You should have seen the way she was looking at Lawson," and, "I bet she's run off for some nasty with him," and—poking two fingers under his ribs—"Ricky P. can't even keep track of his own girlfriend."

She listened silently and hoped he'd talk himself out, but this tactic didn't seem to be working well. The longer she was quiet, the more paranoid Ricky became.

"Don't you understand, Britney?" he said, his green eyes wide and pleading. "I love you."

She liked that he loved her, she *loved* that he loved her, but she didn't like hearing it in this horrible begging way.

"You're drunk," she said.

"That doesn't mean I don't love you."

She tried to tune him out. They'd been sitting in front of her father's house for half an hour, and she was starting to become afraid that they'd never stop fighting. She gazed at the street. The city had re-paved it last summer, and it was such a glimmering shade of black that it looked slick even when it was dry.

Despite the fact that the heat was running full blast, Ricky's car was icy cold. It was an old green Honda with over a hundred thousand miles on it. In warm weather, it smelled like mildew, but now it just smelled like cold. The cracks in the plastic on the dashboard seemed to grow in this weather. She didn't understand why he couldn't get a new one. Anything would be better than this junker.

She shivered and tugged Ricky's giant letter jacket, its sleeves hanging down past her fingertips, tighter around her, afraid that she might have to give it back soon. Nuzzling her nose in the collar, she picked up faint whiffs of Obsession for Men and hair gel. Quintessential Ricky smells.

She stared out the window of the old car and thought about

how nice it would be to finally be allowed to get out of the car and go inside the house, where it was warm.

"I love you too," she whispered, her mouth tight, her lips thin, the skin of her cheeks taut and tense.

The house, with its white shutters and the pale gray stonework around the doorway, reminded her, as always, of a great old cottage plopped down in the middle of a wide empty plain. Green Pastures was a newish development on the west side of town, and though there were trees, they were all still so small that they had to be supported by stakes. In the winter, the snowdrifts nearly covered them over. The spindly tips of the trees' trunks poked out of the center of weird moonscape craters.

"So . . . so . . . so why can't we . . ."

And now he sounded like he was going to cry. Hockey players aren't supposed to cry, she thought. He hadn't cried when his pit bull, Spur, died. He hadn't cried when he'd almost failed trigonometry and been put on academic probation—and he'd had to miss most of last year's season for that. Why was he crying now? Did getting her answer immediately really matter *that* much to him?

"Just . . . w-w-w-why can't . . . I mean, Britney . . . Britney . . . it just seems like . . ."

He was blubbering. His face, usually so chiseled, was puffy. His lips curled like those of a fish gasping for air.

"Listen, Ricky, I'll have to think about it. But I'm not mad at you, 'kay? And you, don't be mad at me either. Please?" she asked. She *was* mad at him, but if she could just get out of the car, she'd get over it.

She liked being his girlfriend. She'd dreamed about it for years, ever since the two of them were in eighth grade and she was a full foot taller than him. He'd looked so cute playing for the JV team. She'd been such a nerd then. She'd played French horn in the band and said things like "gosh darn it" and "fudge" when she thought she was going to curse.

Smoothing his hand between her two palms, she said, "Let's talk about it tomorrow."

The look he gave her—she couldn't tell if he was going to scream at her or try to kiss her. He did neither, just stared at her forlornly, and she slowly pulled her hands back to her lap.

"Okay?" she said. "Just . . . don't be mad?"

He laughed bitterly.

"No, I mean it, okay?" she said, trying to look deep into his eyes. But as soon as her eyes caught his, he turned away to stare at his own reflection in the windshield.

"So, good night," she said, opening the door.

His tousled hair, frosted blond with brown roots, sparkled in the strong moonlight. Shadows accentuated his cheekbone, which pulsed as he clenched and unclenched his teeth. She wanted to reach across and touch his face one more time, but she didn't.

Instead, she stepped out onto the curb and slammed the door—maybe a little too hard. The sound rattled like a gunshot across the empty street.

Ricky didn't seem to notice. He kept staring at the windshield, his cheek pulsing like it did when he was trying to keep his emotions from bursting out.

Just as she was about to turn to go, he rolled down the window, reached across, and grabbed her wrist. "Wait . . . Britney, I—"

"Tomorrow, okay?" she said, pulling her arm away. "Bye." She crouched down and waved at him. But he didn't move.

"Goodbye," she said again.

He nodded stiffly, and that was enough for her. She turned, her blond hair flying behind her, and marched toward the front door. She heard him turn the ignition over.

"Oh, hold on," she said. She turned and ran toward the car. "I need my CD."

He pressed the eject button and handed it to her—the rock classic *Led Zeppelin IV,* the one with "Stairway to Heaven" on it. They'd listened to the song about two hundred times that first night in her bedroom when her father had been away meeting with a client in Milwaukee.

"Thank you!" she said, surprising herself with the sickly sweet voice she usually reserved for Mr. Massey when she wanted him to give her an extension on her English paper.

Resisting the urge to turn around, she walked slowly away, lingering until she heard him pump the gas. His tires buzzed like chain saws as they spun on the ice, and then he caught traction on a dry spot and the car jerked forward, squealing. He fishtailed for a moment and then he was off down the street.

With Ricky gone, Britney's emotions came flooding to the

surface. She was more upset than she'd realized. Enraged, really. And sad.

Even though she was cold, she didn't want to go inside. The chilly air made her more alert, cleared her mind. She'd lived with cold weather her entire life and she didn't mind it. Instead, she stood on the front stoop and stared out at the snowdrifts. She needed to talk to someone who might understand. Shivering, Britney pulled out her cell phone and scanned through the names in her address book.

Her heart was racing. After two twirls through the list, she found the name she could trust. She hit send and waited for the voice that would come to her rescue.

"Hi," she whispered. "It's me."

three

Ricky was driving too fast. To get out of Britney's development, he first had to navigate through the cove of looping cul-de-sacs, and as he hit the first turn, he almost spun out of control. His wheels locked up and he slid toward the snowbank. His brakes didn't have any effect at all. Somehow he got the car to stop sliding and he sat there for a minute, trying to calm himself down.

The first few times he'd been here to see Britney, he'd gotten lost in the maze of streets, some of which didn't even have street signs yet. Now he knew: Take the first right, then another right at the top of the slope. Stay on this street until it dead-ends at Pine Crest and then take a left and you're out. But tonight each of these turns was treacherous. He was still a little buzzed from the Old Milwaukees he'd pounded at Troy's party. He was going to have to take it slow.

Ricky lived five miles away from Britney, on the opposite side of town. Once he was out of her neighborhood, he swung onto Cedar Street and down past Green Haven Country Club, skirting the outer edge of the UW campus. Now that he was on a major thoroughfare, the street was salted. He sped up a little, but still rattled by his spin in Britney's development, he kept himself five miles under the speed limit.

The quickest route home was to cut across the Washington Avenue strip that ran along the northwest side of town and speed past the fast-food restaurants, warehouse stores, and strip malls. The lights were coordinated there: hit the first and you could cruise through the others as well, all the way home. And it meant that he didn't have to crawl through downtown, where the cops were always out in search of college students they could nab for drunk driving.

A pickup truck with its high beams on turned in behind him as he rolled past the multiplex. Annoyed, he flicked the rearview mirror into tint mode and sped up.

When Ricky stopped for a red light, the pickup pulled right up behind him. He noticed that it was swerving quite a bit. It crept up on his bumper as if the driver were playing fast and loose with the brake—as if the driver were drunk. In the street-lights, Ricky could make out that it was an old Ford, red and rusty. This town was full of them. Every farmer in Wisconsin seemed to have an old red Ford pickup. The front license plate was iced over with thick white frost.

Almost out of gas, Ricky veered across the street into

SuperAmerica when the light turned green. He rattled to an abrupt stop and hopped out the door to run inside and pay the attendant.

Before he was two steps away from the car, the sound of the pickup's revving engine startled him. He turned—too late— and saw that it had jumped the curb and was gunning straight for him.

He fumbled with the door handle, which suddenly seemed to be a complicated device that he couldn't remember how to operate. The closer the truck came, the more confusing the door handle got.

When the truck was almost on top of him, he gave up on the door handle and tried to run toward the attendant's window— he slipped in his sneakers; it was hard even to walk. He couldn't make it out of the way fast enough. The truck rammed into him, crunched into his car with a sound like thunder, knocking it into the gas pump. It barreled back onto the road, dragging Ricky along with it, his arms splayed across the hood, his feet bouncing along the road.

Gas spewed from the pump like water from a hydrant. It soaked into the snowbank, turning it into a dirty yellow sludge. The attendant working the cash register ran out to see what had happened, but by the time he got there, the pickup was just two tiny dots of red in the darkened distance. He was the only witness, and he had seen nothing. A red truck spun out of control; that's all he could tell the police later. The same one everyone had.

As the truck sped off, Ricky's body gradually slipped under its chassis. His jeans caught and ripped on the rough pavement, and as they pulled away, his skin began to chafe as well. The muscles began to tear from his body. A bloody trail of unidentifiable body parts was strewn out in the truck's wake.

Finally, three blocks later, Ricky's torso slipped and spun under the pickup's rear right wheel, but the truck roared on, leaving Ricky where he fell in a twisted heap. A mangled raccoon on the side of the road, his blood creeping slowly into the ice.

four

Thank God, Britney's best friend, Melissa, was home. They talked for twenty minutes about the argument Britney had just had with Ricky. Their conversation was filled with all the details of the party and the car ride home.

"It's not like I want to break up with him," Britney said into her cell. "I just get so mad when he's drunk like that and then I start acting bitchy. I can't help it." She sat on the steps leading to the front door, gazing at the cliffs of snow along the edge of the driveway. The Montgomerys across the street had installed a freestanding basketball hoop at the edge of their driveway, and it looked terribly lonely in the moonlight.

"Where is he now?"

"Probably at home."

"Well, don't call him tonight. I've been reading this psych

21

book about power dynamics, and I can tell you right now, if you call him, you'll lose the advantage. He needs to call first and apologize to you for acting like such a jackass."

Melissa was a carryover from when Britney had been unpopular, the only one of her old friends she still talked to. She was embarrassed now about some of her old friends—Bobby Plumley, for instance—but Melissa was different. Melissa knew her almost as well as her father did. The two of them had met when they were in second grade. They'd taken a modern dance class together at the Madison Voices and Visions Children's Resource Center. Throughout middle school and the first few years of high school, they were both in the advanced math and English classes, but last year Britney had stopped studying to build her social life, and Melissa had gone on to place into the freshman comp-lit class at the University of Wisconsin. Britney still trusted her with almost everything.

"What you should do, I think," Melissa went on, "is give it a day. Let both of you simmer down and get some perspective. If you really love each other, a day away won't hurt anything."

"Yeah, I guess. If you love something, set it free and all that, right?"

"Exactly," said Melissa, and she spontaneously broke into the old Sting song—"*If you want to keep something precious, you got to lock it up and throw away the key. . . .*"

This made Britney laugh, and by the time she hung up, she was no longer angry. Instead, she was sad that she and Ricky seemed to have more fights than fun together. She lingered outside and tried to remember all the great times she'd shared with Ricky.

For instance, there was that school-sponsored brat fest on Lake Mendota, where they'd first gotten together at the end of last year. There'd been a bonfire along the rocky shoreline, and as it died out, everyone had headed over to Troy's for the after party. One of the few people left stirring the embers, she was standing there, feeling sort of lonely and wishing she had somebody to talk to, when he'd come up beside her. She could still remember odd the way his white-and-green Packers baseball cap rode so low on his forehead that she was surprised he could see where he was going. He'd grinned at her and almost chivalrously taken the hat off, bending it back and forth to preserve the crease.

"What're you smiling about?" she had said.

"Nothing, just . . . you look like your mom just died or something."

"That's not funny," she'd said, making the beady-eyed look that she'd perfected after years of fending off the barbs of people who thought they were better than her.

"Oh, damn, you're the one whose mom really did die, aren't you?"

"Uh—yeah."

"I'm sorry." The mortified expression on his face told her he wasn't pretending. Then very softly, he'd said, "I know it's not the same, but I lost a good friend this year too."

"Really?"

"Sabrina Reynolds."

Sabrina, the cheerleading captain, had been killed the previous spring behind the Hardee's where she worked on the weekends. Her body had been found in the Dumpster and she had been stabbed thirty-four times.

"I didn't know you and Sabrina were close." Britney's carefully plucked eyebrows rose in concern.

"Oh, we didn't date or anything like that, but we were . . . She was a bud of mine."

"I'm sorry to hear that," Britney said.

Sabrina had been the second student from La Follette to die last year. The week before school started, Danny Boyle, a friend of Bobby Plumley's whom Britney had sometimes hung out with, had been found hanging from a noose in his grandparents' barn. Britney didn't like to talk about the deaths. They depressed her. She awkwardly tried to change the subject. "So, was there some reason you came here to talk to me?"

"Yeah, so listen." As he spoke, the flayed fingertips of his two hands bounced against each other. "I was thinking that you could hang out with me at the Union this Thursday. It's the first day of Music on the Lake, and some group called The Wunderkind is playing. I think they're a polka band or something like that."

As what he'd said sank in, she began to giggle at its absurdity. Why would someone like him want to date her? Her giggles grew into great guffaws. She laughed so hard her gut began to ache.

"I guess that's a no, huh?" he said.

Holding her breath until she got herself back under control, she held up a finger as if to say "Wait a sec." Able to talk again, she said, "I didn't say no."

Or the evening that he'd taken her out to Giovanni's, the fanciest restaurant in town, and presented her with a beautiful friendship ring—a modest opal centered on silver. She had it on right now! That was the night of their first kiss. She could still remember the way his lips had tasted, salty and warm with a slight touch of tomato.

So many moments they'd shared together.

Gazing at the CD in her hand, Britney remembered the night back in July when it had become so special to her. "Stairway to Heaven." She'd put it on auto-replay on the centralized stereo that fed to speakers all over the house. Then she'd led Ricky by the hand up the stairs, into her room, and they'd done things she'd waited her whole life to do, things she'd promised herself she wouldn't do unless the time was perfect and the boy was perfect and the future was assured of being perfect too.

The tears, once they started, just wouldn't stop. They froze to her face, stinging and deepening the chill in her bones. When her bottom lip quivered, it rattled against her teeth like an ice cube, and numb, it seemed to hold the contorted shape of her sadness. Her whole body heaved and shuddered with each new wave of emotion. The cold merely egged on the convulsions. She felt like something outside herself had taken control of her body and was now shaking it with furious might.

She couldn't go inside, not now, not like this. Her father was usually asleep by this time, but Adam was probably awake.

Adam was the son of Steven Saft, Britney's dad's old U. of Penn law school buddy. Two months ago, he'd been shipped here from their home in New Hampshire to shield him from what her father called his parents' "misunderstanding." At least, that was the official story. He had other problems too, but Britney's father wouldn't tell her what these were.

She'd picked up enough to know that he'd gotten in some sort of serious trouble, but she had no idea what it could be. To her, he seemed more like a geek than a deadbeat. She couldn't imagine him being bold enough to do anything really dangerous. Right now, he was most likely logged on to his computer playing EverQuest or whatever it was he did up there. He'd been in Madison for two months now, and it seemed like all he did was play that game. She definitely didn't want him to see her like this.

She wiped the wet mascara from her cheeks and pulled her hair back into a bright yellow binder. She dug her brush out of her black imitation Kate Spade bag and stroked it through her ponytail a few times. Then she double-checked her face in her compact mirror, carefully daubing the streaks of black from her cheeks.

Her pink snow boots were sopping wet, so before going inside, she slipped them off her feet. The protocol was to carry them to the bathroom and let them dry off in the tub. Otherwise they'd create big puddles and warp the hardwood floors.

The foyer was full of shadows. The dark outline of the chandelier above her head seemed to hang especially low tonight, as if there might be something heavy sitting in it.

On tiptoes, she tried to sneak upstairs as quietly as she possibly could.

The shadows wavered and quaked like there was something alive, a person lurking in them.

A voice came from the darkness. "Britney?"

"Wha—" She jumped. Her boots thudded to the floor.

"You've been sitting out front a long time, haven't you?"

It was her father. Sitting in the shadows in the hard-back chair they kept next to the small antique table in the foyer.

"Can you turn on the light or something?" she said. "You scared me to death!"

She swiped at the light switch and illuminated the room. Her dad's face was long, his nose pointy and shrewd. His exceptionally long, thin legs stuck out into the middle of the room. He wasn't that old, but his hair had turned shock white after Britney's mom had died. Tonight he looked especially pale under the bushy wings of his eyebrows, and Britney knew he was worried about something. On the table next to his large, meaty hand sat a telltale glass of ice cubes melting into the dregs of what had been scotch. He collected single malts but only drank them when he was either trying to impress guests or was upset about something and unable to sleep. Usually he drank cheaper stuff.

"It's really cold out there," he went on, "but you didn't want to come in."

Britney shrugged.

"Because you and Ricky had a big fight." He arched his

right eyebrow. "I could see you through the window. What did I tell you about him and his friends? You're such a smart girl, Brit. And so sensitive. I really . . . it baffles me why you want to be with a guy like that."

He kept his voice soothing and controlled, but his disdain for Ricky still came through loud and clear. He'd been against the relationship from the very start. To his mind, Ricky and his friends were nothing more than thugs. It especially irked him that because they were among the star jocks in town, when they were caught drinking or fighting, the police gave them preferential treatment.

She tried to find something to look at that would conveniently hide her face from him. Though she'd cleaned up, there was no erasing the redness that her tears had coaxed to the surface of her eyes.

Taking her chin softly in his hand, he turned her face up toward his so he could look at her.

"What happened?" he said.

He was such a kind man and so many things had gone badly for him. Britney's mom, Jan, had accidentally drowned while they were white-water rafting up near the Wisconsin Dells—her body had never been found—breaking his heart and filling him with an unshakable loneliness. As if that weren't enough, Jan had also run his law office. He was a prominent Madison defense attorney, and keeping track of everything was too much for him to do alone. It took him a year, but he'd eventually had to go hire someone new, a recent college grad named Tamara

Lederer. Now, even eleven months since she started, this batty girl still hadn't mastered the filing system.

Britney had seen the strain it put on him. The harrowed eyes. The way he picked at his food. She hated to burden him with her problems with Ricky.

"Nothing happened," she said, and gave him a weak smile.

"Something must have happened, Britney. It's right there on your face. Wet cheeks, raccoon eyes. Something's definitely wrong. I don't know what—and I won't unless you tell me, but I can tell it's something." He measured out an inch of space with his fingers. "I've known you since you were this big, Britney. I've become pretty good at recognizing these things." As an afterthought, he added, "And that frown looks like it needs to be turned upside down."

"You're sweet," she said.

"You're not going to tell me, are you?"

"It's nothing. Just . . . Ricky."

"What about Ricky?"

Britney paused. She wasn't sure exactly what to say. "He—nothing," she said finally.

Looking meaningfully into her eyes, he said, "You should tell me when something's upsetting you. I can help more than you think."

He held her gaze for what seemed like too long. She turned away first, stared at the photo of the family that hung on the wall leading up the stairwell: all three of them, Mom, Dad, and her, wearing their matching Christmas sweaters, the ones with the corny knit panda bears on them, posed with stiff smiles in front of the fireplace.

"We just had a fight, that's all. We—I'll be fine."

"Well, if you won't tell me, will you let me give you a hug anyway?"

His arms felt like heavy weights around her waist, but they still comforted her. She burrowed her face into his chest. He knew her so well.

She was crying again.

five

A rapping at her bedroom door woke her up the next morning. She hoped that if she just ignored it, maybe she could roll over and fall back asleep. The sadness she'd felt when she'd gone to bed had lingered and sunk into her bones in the night.

"Britney! Enough already! For the hundredth time, do you have any idea what time it is?"

"Sort of," she mumbled.

Peering with one half-closed eye at the Peanuts clock she'd had on her wall since she had learned to tell time, she saw it was already 11 a.m.

When her father stuck his head around her door, she had to scramble for the blankets so he wouldn't catch her naked.

"Jesus, Dad!"

He stepped inside and leaned against the wall. He was wearing his yard work clothes: faded jeans and a green-and-white rugby shirt.

"Are you up yet?"

"Now I am!"

"Good. And are you feeling any better?" He smiled softly, but she could tell it was fake.

She snuggled into her covers, balled them in her fists up under her chin. "No," she said bluntly.

Moving right to the point, he said, "Well, I need you up now. I want you to take Adam downtown in, oh—" He glanced at his watch. "I actually wanted you to be gone by now, but let's say half an hour. His parents and I have decided he needs to find a job."

"Ugh." She hid her head under the blanket and squirmed.

"I can't do it, Britney. And whatever it is between the two of you, I need you to get over it. He's a troubled kid."

"I know he's a troubled kid. Last time he was here, he chased me around that berry farm we went to with a dead mole."

"Last time he was here, the two of you were only nine years old. And even if you think he is annoying, you're the mature one. You can handle it. Let's go." Clapping, he said, "He's waiting for you."

"Fine. Whatever," she said, and her father left her alone again.

Adam didn't know anybody in Madison and he didn't know how things worked here. From the day Britney had been told he was coming to stay with them, she'd worried that he'd cramp her style. He was funny looking, maybe not pimply, but too skinny for his height. He dressed preppy—that might go over all right in New Hampshire, but it was the furthest thing from cool in Wisconsin. Light blue Tommy Hilfiger oxfords and pleated khakis and beat-up old running shoes. Instead of the heavy insulated parkas everyone around here wore to keep out the winter wind, he wore a canvas Lands' End hunting jacket. He parted his floppy hair on the side. In New Hampshire, he'd apparently been a star on the golf team. *The golf team!* That was like being the star of the chess club. When he walked, his elbows and knees bopped around as if someone had taken the joints out of them.

And there was something awkward and unpleasant about him. He had a malicious way of teasing her, pestering her for no reason, long after she told him to leave her alone.

Now, as he sat next to her in the passenger seat of the bright yellow VW Bug that her father had bought her for her sixteenth birthday—the new kind with the wrapping, oversized aerodynamic windows and the thing on the dash designed to hold flowers—he kept asking her questions as if he were doing research or something. "How many people live in Madison?" "Besides cheese and milk and stuff, what other industries do you have here?" "Is it true people here drink more beer than the whole rest of the country combined?"

Her stock answer to all of these questions was, "I don't know." She couldn't fathom why these things mattered to him—unless he was just being willfully annoying, which would make sense; that's how he usually was.

"I've heard there's a wicked rock scene here. Are there any cool bands I should check out right now?"

She turned on the radio. "I don't *know,* Adam," she said. "Why don't you scan the channels for a while and see?"

"I mean underground stuff that doesn't make the radio. The stuff you can only pick up on the QT."

"I have no idea." This was getting frustrating. She flicked the radio back off and turned onto Cedar.

"You don't know? How could you not know?" He was smirking. She could tell he was looking for an excuse to argue with her.

"Because I don't. Music's just music. I've got lots of things I'd rather do with my time than try to keep up with bands nobody's ever heard of."

"How can you say that! Music's everything! And in Madison . . . I mean Rot Gut's from Madison!"

"I don't even know what Rot Gut is."

He groaned.

"Rot Gut's this legendary band from, like, I don't know, the late eighties, early nineties. They were Satanists. They dug up grave sites and stuff. They were cool as hell."

"That's pleasant," she said.

She couldn't understand how he'd tricked her into another tedious argument like this, but she could have predicted it would happen. He did it every time. Now she was rattled. She wasn't paying attention to the road. "Adam, it's really icy. I need to concentrate on my driving."

"I just can't believe you've never heard of them. I mean, they're counterculture gods. And they're from Madison."

They were in the university district now, driving the past redbrick dorms and the large stately buildings that housed the various campus departments.

"Hey, which one's the economics building?" Adam asked.

"I don't know. Why?"

"Stan Chen."

Here he went again. "Look, I'm sick of this game, Adam. Either tell me or don't."

"That guy who shot up all those people in '97. He was a student in the economics department. He took over one of the classrooms."

Now she remembered. It had been a huge thing. Something to do with the guy's PhD funding or something. She didn't like thinking about it. Murder and death always sent her thoughts off toward her mother.

"I can understand you not knowing who Rot Gut is, but Stan Chen? It was such a huge thing. It made the national news. I even heard about it in New Hampshire," Adam said.

"Can we talk about something else?" she said. She was absorbed now in memories of that fateful white-water-rafting trip. The last time she'd seen her mother smile, adjusting the straps on her orange life vest. "Now I feel *completely* safe," she'd said with a laugh.

An SUV in the opposing lane began honking at them hysterically, waking Britney from her reverie. In her peripheral vision, she saw someone frantically motioning at her, but she couldn't tell who it was. The SUV sped by so fast that Britney didn't get a good look at it, just a blur of blue and black.

"Hey, wasn't that your cheerleader friends?"

In the rearview mirror, she could make out the back end of the SUV. A baby blue Ford Explorer. It could have been Erin's car.

"I don't know, was it?"

"They looked really upset. I bet someone broke a nail."

It just figured that Adam would distract her so much that she'd miss her own friends. She wondered what they had been trying to tell her. "Thanks for letting me know," she said flatly.

"I did let you know."

"Yeah, after they were already past."

"I'm sure, whatever it was, it was really important," Adam said. He jumped into a high, mocking girly voice and said, "Oh my God! You'll never guess what Buffy told me last night! Did you know that Biff—"

The light changed, and Britney pounded the gas in frustration. The car fishtailed briefly and then sped forward.

"Whoa!" said Adam, his voice back to normal. "Who are you now, Jeff Gordon?"

She'd had as much as she could take from him.

Screeching the car to a halt, she said, "You know what? Get out. We're close enough to downtown. You can walk from here."

That shut Adam up, but it didn't wipe the smirk off his face.

"I'm serious," she said.

Their stare-down didn't last long because Adam started chuckling to himself.

"Sure. All right. Cool," he said with a shrug. "I'll catch you later."

He ambled out of the car as though nothing had happened and obnoxiously threw her the peace sign as he walked away.

Britney sped off. She was preoccupied with the hockey wives, worried about what she'd missed. They must have been trying to get her attention for some reason. She wished she could call them, but she'd forgotten her cell phone. And by now there was no way of knowing where they'd be.

At least there was Melissa. It was doubtful that she'd know the dirt since she didn't have any connection with that crowd, but at least Britney could complain about Adam to her. And she might have some more good advice about Ricky.

six

Melissa's house was in a transient section of town right near the UW campus. Most everybody who lived there were college students and weirdos. It wasn't unusual to see them having snowball fights in their underwear or smoking pot out on their front porches. The houses were a hodgepodge of styles, a lot of duplexes and two-story nondescript apartment buildings, the paint peeling, old furniture piled in the yard. Reggae music or, worse, jazz could be heard coming from the different buildings at all hours of the night and day. The streets were lined with cars so old and beat up that Britney always wondered if they'd been abandoned. The trees, elms and oaks and chestnuts, were large and shady, and when their leaves turned yellow and began to blanket the ground, you could almost feel the education in the air.

When she arrived at Melissa's pale blue clapboard house, Britney stormed right in without bothering to knock. That was the kind of friendship they had. They were like sisters—or they had been until this year. Britney had grown a little apart from Melissa, not because she wanted to; she was just so busy now with Ricky and all the new friends she'd made through him. Melissa's parents were professors at the university, and she had inherited their awesome intelligence.

"It's you!" said Melissa when she saw Britney standing in the doorway. Britney let Melissa pull her inside.

The house was a mess as always. Every surface—the coffee table, the end table, the plush cushioned chair as well as the rocking chair, and even the floor—was buried by papers and books. The bookshelves were full, and whatever space wasn't packed with bits of text was cluttered with the knickknacks Melissa's mother collected on her travels throughout the third world. Britney stared at an abstract painting, an ugly canvas covered in blobs of thick brown and green and purple paint. Supposedly it had been painted by someone famous, but Britney had never heard of the artist. As far as she was concerned, it was, like so much of the stuff in Melissa's house, junk.

Melissa's red hair frizzed out in unruly curls and she hid her eyes behind studious cat's-eye glasses. She could be cute, Britney was sure of it, if she just tried a little, but instead she clomped around in beat-up combat boots and wore shapeless overalls and lumpy sweaters in all the worst colors.

"I've been trying to call you all day, but your dad said you were out. Is there something wrong with your cell phone?"

"I forgot it at home."

"I figured." Melissa held Britney's hand out in front of her and looked her up and down as if she were searching for a hidden message. "Are you okay?"

"I don't know. I guess I just wanted to be alone today."

Releasing Britney's hand, Melissa let the topic drop. "You're really upset, huh?"

"I *am* upset. I've been carting that idiot Adam all over town and I ran into the other hockey wives—"

"It probably doesn't help that you were fighting with Ricky right before it happened."

Britney shuddered.

"Let's not talk about that," she said, suddenly repulsed by the idea of rehashing last night with Melissa again.

She felt dizzy.

"I mean, it's going to be harder for you to find closure now," said Melissa.

"Yeah, I know," said Britney.

Her pulse pounded in her temples, and she held her hand to her head to stop the spinning. Just as suddenly as the dizziness had started, it stopped. "Wait a minute, what are you talking about?"

Melissa gasped. Her eyebrows rose above the frames of her glasses. "You don't know, do you? You seemed so upset, I thought you knew. He's . . . Britney, he's dead. Ricky's dead."

The sage, schoolmarmish expression that Melissa usually

wore slowly drained away as Britney stared at her. Pushing a pile of newspapers out of the way, Britney sank onto the pullout couch. She looked around the room in search of something simple to focus on, but there was nothing simple in Melissa's house.

Britney grew very quiet. She curled up into a tight ball on the couch and pulled Ricky's letter jacket close around her. She fingered the small brass hockey stick that was affixed to the rough-textured *L* on the jacket. The letter was right over her heart.

"I'm sorry," said Melissa.

The two of them sat in shocked silence for a while until out of nowhere, Britney asked with a voice that was surprisingly steady given what she'd just been told, "How did it happen?"

"He was killed."

"How?"

"A hit and run. He must have been driving home from dropping you off. It happened at right about the same time as when we were talking on the phone. They're saying it was a drunk-driving accident."

Britney gasped. "He hit someone?"

"Someone hit him. His car was parked at a gas station. The driver swerved off the road and . . . and dragged him."

"Do they know who killed him?"

"Somebody driving a red pickup truck. That's all they know. Or that's all they're saying, anyway."

Britney bobbed her head like she was in a trance.

Then she laughed. She laughed so hard that the laughter bent her over, clenching her stomach, squeezing tears from her eyes. She laughed and laughed and she couldn't stop laughing. When finally she got herself under control, she looked up at Melissa and grinned ruefully.

"You think this is funny?" Melissa looked horrified. Her head was pulled back as though in shock at having seen Britney turn suddenly into a person she didn't know.

"No," said Britney. "No. I'm . . . I was just thinking. If we hadn't had that big fight, I would have been with him. That old Ford would have probably hit me as well as him. I'd be dead too."

Melissa frowned, but Britney's pleading eyes reached out toward her and she moved close and held her friend tight.

seven

Adam lit a cigarette, his first of the day, and contemplated his various employment options. If he had to work, he wanted to at least work at a cool store.

Kicking along State Street, he took in the sights. Since arriving in Madison, he'd been up and down this street numerous times, and he always compared it to his memory of what the street had been like back when he'd come to visit as a kid.

He still had a hard time getting used to the college bars that had proliferated in the past eight years. Long Tall Sally's and Kegger's and The Watering Hole. They weren't crowded now, but he imagined that they would fill up with Greeks and girls gone wild—people like Britney and that obnoxious guy she dated, Ricky—once the sun started to set.

In his memory, this street had stood out as an exotic never

land where people in dreadlocks, reeking of patchouli, lingered in front of dark, tapestry-shrouded stores called things like The Mad Hatter and Liquid Sky.

One time, during his visit to Madison when he was nine, he and Britney came down here with their families. They'd wandered up and down the street for a while, taking in the sunshine and warmth of the day. There had been some sort of farmers' market, and that was why they were there: the grown-ups had wanted to buy homemade jams or something. But to him, the farmers' market hadn't been as interesting as all the weird people up and down the street.

While the adults looked at the vegetable stands, he and Britney wandered off together to find something more interesting. A shirtless guy with long hair and batik pants had been playing acoustic guitar on a bench and, Adam remembered, he'd wanted to join the small circle of people listening to him.

Britney was scared of the guy, though—at that time, she'd seemed scared of most everything. When Adam asked her why, she said, "He's dirty."

"You're dirty," Adam said.

She glared at him. "I'm not dirty," she said.

"Your mom told me you were dirty."

This had made her cry. He felt bad, thinking back on it. Her mother had been an odd, nervous woman. And now she was dead. At the time, though, he hadn't been able to resist the urge to get under Britney's skin. It was too easy. She always took things so much more seriously than they needed to be taken. In that regard, she hadn't changed.

As he wandered up the street, he kept an eye out for places he remembered from his earlier visit. The ethnic restaurants were still there: Mamood's Shawarma, Zulu Ethiopian Cuisine, Rayne's Macrobiotic Burrito Stand, but for every one of these, there was a chain restaurant too: Quiznos, Chipotle, Johnny Rockets, Wendy's.

He knew exactly where he wanted to work: Amoeba Records, if it was still around. Approaching the corner where he remembered it having been, he was relieved to see the big drippy Day-Glo sign still there, a little worse for wear, but he could deal with that.

He leaned against the counter and filled an application form out on the spot. In answer to the question asking what music he liked, he said, *Air, Tricky, and old-school hip-hop, especially Kurtis Blow. Mos Def is pretty good too.* He hoped this would impress them. When the form asked him what music he didn't like, he said, *Anything that's not real.* He figured they'd know what he meant. And as for why he wanted to work here, he said, *Because Amoeba's the coolest record store in town.* A little kissing up never hurt anyone.

The guy behind the counter was dressed in a retro-seventies style. Hip-hugger rust-colored polyester pants. A tuxedo T-shirt. His mop of hair hung down so far into his eyes that Adam couldn't believe he could see through it. He nodded as he read Adam's application, though, and when he was done, he said, "Air's cool, but London Underground are cooler."

Adam was pretty sure that the guy's dismissive tone was his way of showing that he was impressed, so in response Adam shrugged. "Yeah, they're all right too," he said, even though he'd never heard their music.

Then the guy said, "So, can you start tomorrow?" and Adam grinned.

"Yeah. Absolutely."

Back out on the street, he felt the need to walk out his excitement. He walked past Ragstock used clothing and Big Billy's Brat Shop and a store called Essence that specialized in scented candles. On and on he walked, three, four, five blocks, and while he was walking, he thought about Britney and her cliquey friends. Now that he was an Amoeba employee, he had certifiable proof that he was a hundred times better than they thought he was. He could only imagine how upset she would be when she heard that he'd pulled off this coup.

State Street was only eight blocks long. It started at the edge of the UW campus and ran on a diagonal until it dead-ended at the lush, expansive capital lawn. He could see the marble dome up ahead, and he wondered if he should call Ed Johnson and ask him to pick him up. He didn't want to. He was enjoying State Street. At Mr. Johnson's house, there wasn't much to do but IM his golf buddies back home, and that just reminded him how much he missed them.

Coming up on the end of the street, he stopped in front of the Camara Theatre, a regal old movie palace that had passed its prime. The marquee was missing lights. The red carpet that spread from the front door to the street had long ago been worn threadbare. He was surprised it was still there. In Manchester, New Hampshire, where he was from, all the theaters like this one had been torn down years ago and replaced by multiplexes.

A black-and-white poster out front proclaimed that the theater was having a horror festival. Over the next two weeks, they would be showing *The Exorcist, The Omen, Children of the Corn, Carrie, Halloween,* and about thirty other screamers. Today was *Psycho.*

Adam had never seen it. He remembered reading something in *Premiere* magazine last year about how the movie was based on a real-life serial killer, a guy named Ed Gein, who, Adam knew, was from Wisconsin. He thought it would be kind of cool to watch a bit of spooky mythology about the local culture.

It started at three, in half an hour. He figured he should call Mr. Johnson to let him know he would be home late.

As he fished in the pocket of his green windbreaker for his cell phone, a pair of hands clamped onto his shoulders. He let out a shriek and jumped. He spun around ready to fight.

There, looming uncomfortably close, was a pudgy, pasty guy in a tattered army coat glistening with buttons—a smiley face with a bullet hole in the forehead, a bloodred anarchy symbol, the outline of a hand with the middle finger raised. His hair was styled into a greasy bowl cut, grown out so it hung in daggers over his eyes, which were further hidden behind brown plastic glasses. Underneath his coat, Adam could see a black T-shirt on which had been stenciled the sentence, *Just be glad I'm not your kid*. He was smiling maniacally.

"Scared you, didn't I?" he said. His voice had a high reedy quality to it, as if he had to squeeze it out of his throat.

Taking a deep breath, Adam backed up until he bumped into the wall.

"You're that kid from New Hampshire, right?" the guy said.

Adam wasn't sure what tack to take. He knew he could beat this guy in a fight—in his ugly last few months in New Hampshire, he'd taken much bigger, tougher guys than this—but he wasn't convinced it was worth it. The best thing to do would be to walk away, but the guy's arms were stretched out in front of him, his fingers extended, poised to catch Adam whichever direction he darted.

Tensing and straightening up against the wall, Adam spoke calmly, as if he were talking to a vicious dog. "How'd you know that?"

"New Hampshire's supposed to be almost a nice place to live. Why'd you decide to come to this stinking town?"

"I'm . . ." Adam thought of his parents, of the for-sale sign in the front yard, of the sterile motel where his father was now living. "I'm staying with some friends."

"Oh, yeah?" The guy sneered. "Who?"

"Britney Johnson."

When the guy heard her name, he acted like someone had hit him on the back of the head with a baseball bat. He buckled at the waist and bent almost to the ground. He sounded like he was wheezing. Laughter. Copious laughter.

"I knew that," the guy said through his laughter. "You're Adam Saft. I know all about you."

While the guy was doubled over, Adam took his opportunity to slide out from against the wall. He mumbled to the guy, "You're a freak," and began walking briskly away.

"Hey! Wait! Where you going?" The guy suddenly had him by the elbow. His grip was tight, and Adam began to think he might have underestimated the guy's strength. "We were having an interesting conversation."

"Okay."

"I was going to go see that movie. *Psycho*. You were too, no?"

"What, are you a mind reader now?"

"Oh, come on. I saw you digging in your pocket for money. Don't lie to me. I think we're going to be great friends."

"I doubt that."

Pulling on Adam's elbow, the guy said, "We are. You can count on it. Come on, let's go."

Not feeling like he had any other choice, Adam followed him back toward the ticket counter.

"Britney Johnson. *Little* Britney Johnson." The guy stretched the words out into grotesque balloons and chuckled again. "I'm so sorry you've got to be stuck in a house with her."

Adam couldn't help but smile. There was a teasing quality to this weirdo that was beginning to appeal to him.

"You don't like Britney?" Adam asked.

"Let's say I find her *very* interesting."

"How come?"

"Oh, that's a long story." The guy's mouth twisted into a tortured smile. "I can't tell you that. Not right now. Suffice it to say that we used to be the bestest of buddies, but sadly, all good things come to an end—especially when other people are involved. Ask her about Bobby Plumley when you get home. See what kind of reaction you get."

"That's you?"

"That's me, Bobby Plumley."

Yanking his wallet from the back pocket of his black jeans, Bobby flipped it open and pulled out a twenty.

"This one's on me," he said. Then, turning to the pretty brunette behind the ticket counter, he said, "Two *Psycho*s." And in they went.

eight

The three of them, Britney, her father, and Adam, sat around the kitchen table, eating lasagna. Or, her father and Adam were eating it. Britney just picked at her food, separating the meat from all the other stuff that wasn't on her diet and pushing the food around on her plate. She had no appetite. She was too upset.

Throughout most of the meal, an awkward silence had cloaked the room. Now that the whole household knew about Ricky's death, it was as if he were sitting with them at the table, bloody and disfigured and staring at them with wet, mournful eyes. Of course, he wasn't, but everyone felt his presence anyway and no one knew what to say about it.

Straining to make conversation, Mr. Johnson asked Adam what he'd done this afternoon. The two of them had already talked about this. The real purpose of the question was to provide a neutral topic and a sense of normalcy around the table.

Adam swallowed his bite of lasagna, wiped a strand of mozzarella from his chin, and said, "I went to a movie. *Psycho*."

Britney glanced up at him. The last thing she wanted to hear about right now was *Psycho*. Her father, of all people, should have realized this.

"And he met a friend of yours," her father said with a helpful smile.

"Who?"

Adam tipped his head. "Guess."

"I'm really not in the mood for one of your games," she said.

"Adam, not right now. Just tell her."

"Bobby Plumley."

Britney sat back in her chair and glared at the two of them. Of all the things there were in the world to talk about, she wondered why they had to choose this one.

"Bobby Plumley's *not* my friend," she said.

Her father peered at her from below his bushy eyebrows. "I thought you and Bobby *were* friends. He used to come around the house all the time." She knew he didn't mean to take sides against her, but she couldn't help feeling betrayed by his statement.

"Well, we're not anymore."

Unconsciously, she reached for the hockey pin on Ricky's jacket and traced its shape with her index finger. She hadn't taken the jacket off all day. She never wanted to take it off.

Adam brushed the hair from his face, and she saw a smirk pressing out from the corners of his mouth. "Why not?"

Just thinking about him made her head feel like it had flames shooting out of it. If there was one thing in her life she regretted, it was having spent so much time with Bobby Plumley.

"He's a sociopath, okay? Can we . . ." She broke down in sobs. Pulling Ricky's letter jacket tight, she hugged herself in it. "Can we talk about something else?"

The tortured silence descended again on the table.

After a while, a plaintive sympathy in his voice, Mr. Johnson said to Britney, "If you want to cancel with Dr. Yeager tomorrow, I'll understand."

Britney nodded. "Thanks," she said. Dr. Yeager was the shrink who was theoretically supposed to be helping her deal with her feelings over her mother's death.

After another long silence, he tried again. "When is the funeral, honey?"

"On Wednesday. They're canceling school."

"Well, that's good, at least," said her father.

She couldn't bear it anymore.

"No. No, it's not good," she said. "Nothing's good."

He reached his long bulky fingers out to touch her arm, but she pulled away from him and he instead patted the table. He couldn't comfort her. No one could comfort her.

Jumping up, she ran from the kitchen and took the stairs two at a time toward her bedroom.

This seemed to be where she always ended up. Shut tight in her room all alone. She remembered what it had been like before her life was transformed by Ricky and the hockey wives. So many nights of watching *Law & Order* reruns. So many weekends spent sitting in her bedroom, telling her stuffed frog about her problems. Her father had brought the frog home as a present after his three-week business trip to New York City when she was six. She called the frog Wart, and she often felt like he was her only friend.

How many secrets had she shared with Wart because she couldn't tell anyone else on earth? Wart knew all about her relationship with her mother. He'd comforted her after her mother'd slapped her face when, at eight years old, she'd poured chopped onions into the vanilla ice cream—she'd been just a kid; she hadn't known any better! He knew how much they had fought as she grew into a teenager, but he also knew how much she missed her mother, how bad she felt about the strife that had existed between them now that she was dead.

Where had Wart disappeared to? He'd been a great comfort. Maybe he could console her over Ricky like he had back then over her mother.

She hadn't seen him in months. He had to be in her room somewhere. She rummaged under the bed, pushing aside the shoe box full of photos from her childhood, the rolled-up posters that had plastered her walls when she was on that Hanson kick—she'd been such a kid then. She couldn't find him anywhere.

Finally, giving up, she turned on her i-Mac and fired up her Yahoo Messenger account. Maybe Erin or Jodi or someone would be there.

A pop-up box told her she had four "friends" connected, and she immediately felt a little bit better. That's right, she thought, she had a whole network of friends to comfort her. She didn't need a stupid stuffed frog.

They were talking about Ricky, giving little testimonials:

Sunshine52 [Cindy]: He wasn't like your average jock because underneath the muscles, he could be real tender. I always had sort of a crush on him. (no offense, Britney) ☺

Sweet'n'Sassy [Erin]: Don't tell Troy, but—me too! But I had a crush on him BECAUSE of the muscles.

Sunshine52: He was dreamy.

LittleOne [Jodi]: I remember one time I was helping him with trig and he said, "The thing is, I actually want to learn this stuff, you know?" That said a lot about him, I thought.

Britney typed in, *You don't know how much hearing all this is helping me! Thanx. I couldn't ask for better friends!*

DaffyD [Daphney]: Hey, did you guys hear the rumor?

Sunshine52: What rumor?

Sweet'n'Sassy: There's a rumor going around that I didn't start?

DaffyD: Digger told me that right before the game on Friday, Ricky told him he thought someone wanted to kill him.

Sunshine52: You're joking.

DaffyD: No.

Britney felt like she was about to throw up. *Did he say who?* she typed.

DaffyD: Digger said he wouldn't tell him. He said Ricky told him he could take care of it by himself. They sort of argued about it, I think. Ricky told Digger to keep it a secret. He said he was just telling him in case something happened—he wanted someone to know.

Sweet'n'Sassy: Then it wasn't an accident.

DaffyD: That's what I'm thinking.

It was all too much for Britney. She turned off her computer and sat in the dark, gripped by a fear she hadn't felt since the months immediately after her mother had died.

nine

Instead of holding Ricky's memorial in the auditorium of La Follette High School, which was what had been done for Sabrina Reynolds and Danny Boyle, Mr. Bucholtz, the principal, let the whole school out on Wednesday to attend his funeral in St. Matthew's Church.

St. Matthew's was a cavernous building made of yellow sandstone and designed with lots of ornate arches and an elaborately carved wooden pulpit. Large, brightly colored tapestries illustrating the fruits of the spirit hung on the walls, interspersed with stained glass windows, each one dedicated to a different apostle.

Ricky's casket was displayed on the dais. It was closed—the force of the impact and the unfortunate way he'd been dragged down the street by the truck had left his body a bloody pulp.

His hockey jersey was draped over one end of the casket, and his helmet had been placed over the spot above his head. With this visual clue, Britney could imagine his body inside, cut and bruised and broken. On either side of the casket, two beautiful bouquets of white lilies had been set up.

Britney and her father sat in the front row with Donna Piekowski, Ricky's mother, and his grandparents. His father, Jeff, wasn't there. He and Donna had been high school sweethearts, and she'd gotten pregnant in her junior year. Instead of finishing, she'd dropped out of school and they'd gotten married. When Ricky was four, though, his father had run off to Arizona, leaving his mother to raise him alone. Living with single parents was one of the first things he and Britney had connected over.

Like all Ricky's friends, Britney called his mother Donna. She was only thirty-three years old, but with her streaky blond feathered hair and heavily applied eyeliner, she looked older. She had crow's-feet around her eyes, and her loose off-white blouse and black knee-length skirt hung awkwardly from her body. Even though she was sitting down, she kept fidgeting with the heels of her black stilettos.

Britney felt sorry for Donna. Every time Father Steiger mentioned Ricky's name, Donna sighed loudly and her bald hawkish father shot her a scornful look. She squirmed under his gaze like a child. To make up for this and let her know that she wasn't as alone as she thought she was, Britney held her hand throughout the ceremony.

Watching the mascara streak down Donna's face helped Britney remember the pact she'd made with herself. This morning, as she'd put on her conservative black flower-print dress, Britney had looked at herself in the mirror and said out loud, "Don't be afraid to cry. Today you should be strong and remember the good times, but if ever there was a time and place for tears, this is it. . . . This is what funerals are for." She hadn't cried so far, though; she felt too numb. And she'd already handed almost all the tissues from the travel pack she'd brought along over to Ricky's mom.

After Father Steiger's opening eulogy, there were a variety of speeches.

Mr. Luddy, the hockey coach, went first, describing in short, terse sentences what it felt like the first time he saw Ricky skate, back when he was in sixth grade. "Here was this half-pint of a kid, and who woulda known, he actually had the stuff. Boy, did he ever. He could stop on a dime and his face had this toughness, like he'd mutilate anyone who got in his way. Right then and there, I said to Paul Taube, that kid's going to be unbelievable. I don't care if he's only twelve. He's gonna start for the JV crew."

Mr. Luddy's face gradually turned a bright red and as his speech went on, it seemed to Britney that he wasn't so much mourning Ricky's death as he was mourning the death of his team's chances of winning state again this season.

Next it was Troy's turn. He told a variety of anecdotes. The time his car broke down fifty miles out in the country in the middle of a snowstorm and Ricky drove out to give him a jump. The summer night he'd locked himself out of his house while his parents were out of town and Ricky had helped him break in through the basement window.

This made a certain portion of the crowd chuckle—the hockey players and their wives—and Britney wondered what crazy night he was talking about. It was before her time, that was for sure. She felt jealous, covetous of this exclusive memory.

"And," Troy went on, "Mrs. Robideau, you were right. Ricky did slip me the answers to that trig test last year." Britney's friends laughed again, and again she felt excluded. "I guess to sum up my feelings about Ricky, he was just, you know, a really great guy. He was always there for me."

For a moment, Troy stared out over the heads of the congregation. His heavy brow knotted in what looked to Britney like confusion. Then he ran his thick hand through his longish blond hair—he'd moussed it back into a slick helmet for the funeral—and said, "Thanks." After another moment of confused staring, he burst into tears and shouted, "And whoever did this, I don't care if it was an accident. I don't even care how sorry you feel! We're going to find you and . . ."

Before leaving the podium, he ragefully shook his massive fists in front of him and a shrieking war cry rose from deep in his throat.

Britney was next. From her perch behind the raised wooden podium, she could see how large the crowd truly was. Every pew was jam-packed with people. The La Follette Raccoons, sitting together as a group, took up three whole rows. At the very front swayed The Untouchables, Troy, Digger, and Jeremy, their heads bowed, their arms loosely draped over each other's shoulders. Behind them sat Erin, Cindy, Daphney, and Jodi; they'd all worn identical red T-shirts with the number 43 stenciled on them, Ricky's number. Farther back, a huge slice of the school population had seen fit to pay their respects as well. The crowd was so large that individual faces blurred together, but she recognized a smattering of teachers: Ms. Ahern, Mrs. Rindy, Mr. Bucholtz. There were even people standing up and down the side aisle and a great mass of humanity squished into the back.

Somewhere out there was Adam. He'd been on his own to find a seat because as Britney had explained to her father this morning, "It would be so inappropriate for him to sit up front with the family. He didn't even like Ricky!"

Melissa was out there somewhere as well. Britney couldn't find her, though. She wished she'd asked where Melissa was going to sit. Speaking like this in front of all these people would be much easier if she could look at Melissa while she did it.

Britney had spent all last night writing her speech. She'd done five drafts, getting only so far each time before she became frustrated and scribbled darkly over what she'd written. Finally she'd found what she wanted to say. Unfolding the hand-scrawled speech on the podium in front of her, she looked it over for a long moment.

The church was so silent. Everyone waiting to listen to her.

"Ricky Piekowski," she began, "was my boyfriend. I loved him."

Her voice cracked when she said the word *love*, but she didn't waver. She didn't slow down to collect herself. She had to show the people gathered in the church, she had to show Donna, that she could be strong.

"And he loved me."

She'd reread what she'd written so many times that she knew it by heart. Looking out at all the people whose lives Ricky touched, she went on from memory.

"We only started dating last June, but in the eight months I was lucky to share with him, I got to know him better than I have ever known any other human being. I knew what made him laugh—*The Simpsons*—and what made him frown—the Packers losing to the Vikings. Sometimes when I looked at him, I could tell from the expression on his face exactly what he was thinking—and he always seemed to know what I was thinking too. But we still hadn't discovered everything. There was so much more that we had to learn. We'd barely begun to explore all the things we meant to each other, all the little things that made us who we were.

"And now . . . ?" Her lips clenched into a grimace of tightly controlled pain and sadness. ". . . We never will. I—" Tears began to well in her eyes, but they didn't fall yet. She paused to collect herself.

"I'm sorry," she said. She felt the hot tears slowly begin to drip down her cheeks and wished she hadn't given all her tissues away. "Does someone have a tissue I could have?"

The people in the front row, her father and Donna and Ricky's grandparents and, on the other side of the aisle, The Untouchables glanced at one another and shifted uncomfortably in their seats. For a moment, she thought no one was going to help her. One of the tears had reached the flare of her nostril. It tickled. She admonished herself, Don't wipe it away. Don't use the back of your arm, and waited for some kindness to come her way.

Finally Ricky's grandfather rose from his seat. He had the wide-legged, arthritic gait of an ex–football player. From his lapel pocket, he pulled a monogrammed handkerchief and passed it across the podium to her.

She dabbed at her cheeks with a dainty hand, being careful not to smudge the makeup. Then, bravely returning to her speech, she said, "The night Ricky . . . The night this horrible tragedy took place, Ricky and I had been out celebrating the Raccoons' win over the Prairie Dogs. He'd been so happy. He was a true team player. He didn't want the glory all for himself. He wanted to do what was best for his teammates. He wanted everyone to win. That's what was most important to him. To be part of the group."

Glancing up, she noticed that Digger, Jeremy, and Troy's arms had tightened around one another's shoulders. Their foreheads were pressed hard together, and from the quiver in their bodies, Britney suspected that they were silently sobbing.

"But there was something else about him that night. There was something in the way he smiled at me. He seemed almost bashful. And if you know Ricky, you know he was never bashful."

Mournful, knowing chuckles rose from the crowd.

"Well, here's why."

She reached into the hidden hip pocket of her dress and pulled out a small shimmering object.

"That night, before he dropped me off at home, he gave me this."

She held up the object, a ring, small, unassuming but a ring nonetheless, made of silver and, mounted on it, a diamond.

"He asked me to marry him, to share my life with him. I hadn't said yes yet. I wanted to spend the weekend thinking about it, but . . ." Looking up toward the stone rafters of the church ceiling, Britney said quietly, in a whisper just loud enough for the mike to pick it up, "Yes, Ricky. Yes. I do want to marry you. It's too late now, but my answer would have been yes."

Then she bowed her head and wiped her eyes with the handkerchief Ricky's grandfather had given her.

The air in the church was tense. Everyone was silent, gazing up at her, and she could feel how profoundly deep their sympathy ran. Britney wasn't sure if she should say thank you or what. Her speech was over, but the love that was pressing toward her from the crowd was so great that she didn't want to leave the spotlight.

Donna was supposed to speak next. Britney wasn't looking forward to it. She could already imagine how her speech would go. She'd be surprised if the woman got more than a few words out before she broke down in hysterics. She'd bellow, "Ricky . . . Ricky," maybe say, "My beautiful boy," or, "My only son," or, "Oh God, how could you take him away from me?" Whatever she did, the whole congregation would feel twitchy and be afraid to look at her. No matter how much comfort they threw her way, it wouldn't possibly be enough.

With slow grace and dignity, Britney walked back toward her empty place in the front row pew. The respectful silence emanating toward her filled her with such joy that she almost felt like running up and hugging each and every person there.

Just as she was about to take her seat again, she heard an odd noise coming from the back of the room. A popping sound. A sound of air caught between two palms. Someone was clapping— not the kind of clapping that showed appreciation; sarcastic, ironic clapping, the kind that said, "I'm laughing at you." The gall! And this clapping was gradually getting louder. And faster, like horse hooves picking up speed. Other people were joining in now. They didn't seem to understand that this was a sick joke. They were clapping in earnest, in appreciation. They were clapping because they liked her. She wished they'd stop, though; the thunder of their applause drowned out the instigator, making it impossible for her to pinpoint where the sound had come from.

She plopped down in her seat and covered her face with her hands. She was no longer crying. She didn't even feel sad anymore. She was enraged. Who could possibly show such disrespect for the dead? she wondered. Who could possibly be so out to get her? No. No. She tried to calm herself down with deep-breathing exercises. The more she told herself not to be paranoid, the more paranoid she became.

ten

That night, at the buffet held in Ricky's honor in the VFW hall, the other hockey wives congregated around the head table, where Britney sat with Ricky's family, and ogled her ring.

"It's beautiful!" said Daphney.

They all wanted to know, "Where'd he get it?"

Erin, who could always be counted on to say something just this side of inappropriate, asked, "How'd he *afford* it? He and his mother weren't well-off or anything."

Cindy shushed her and changed the subject. "You two were such a perfect couple," she said.

"Just think what their babies would have looked like," said Daphney, a faraway look sliding over her face.

"Yeah," added Erin, "and just think how much fun Cindy would have had babysitting for them."

Cindy blushed and sighed as if a phantom baby were right there in front of them.

Through all of this, Britney didn't say much. She was still too torn up by her sadness. It made Britney smile to listen to them, though. The sight of them delighting in acting like themselves reminded Britney that the world hadn't completely changed.

Daphney asked, "How'd he do it? I want to hear every detail."

"Well." Britney tried to think back. Time had been moving so slowly since Ricky died that Friday seemed like a lifetime ago. "After we left Troy's party, Ricky drove me to . . ." She searched her mind. "Menominee Park. I didn't want to go. I was tired. I feel bad about it now, but I kept arguing with him about why he wouldn't just take me straight home—"

Erin cut her off. "Get to the good part!" she said. "How did he propose?"

"He made me get out of the car and he led me to a little slope where the snow hadn't been trampled yet. It was so cold, I can't tell you! He made me stand there while he pressed letters into the snow with his body, and it wasn't until he was, like, halfway done that I realized what he was doing."

The other girls sighed and cooed.

"He was spelling it out in the snow!" said Cindy. "That's so romantic."

Britney smiled briefly, but her smile faded as Ricky's face rushed up from her memory.

Though they wanted to, the girls couldn't dwell long over

this story; it was time to join the serving line and they had to return to their tables.

The mood was sad, but it was nice not to have to be sad all alone.

When her mother died, Britney had felt completely isolated. She hadn't even been able to talk to her dad about it because he'd responded by trying to disappear in his work, hiding at the office sometimes until midnight, and, when he could no longer escape, coming home, sitting with his scotch and a look on his face that said, "Please don't come near me; I'll break if you do."

Now, though, she was surrounded, smothered by love. The VFW hall was packed. Thirty large round tables covered in white paper tablecloths. On the center of each table was a bouquet of festive azaleas. Britney couldn't stop imagining that this was what the place would have been like on her wedding night—except on her wedding night, there would have been better music than the soft classical strings piping out of the speakers today. There would have been chinking of glasses and demands, every five minutes, that she and Ricky kiss. They would have held each other tight and danced slowly. And then they would have done the chicken dance and laughed.

The dinner was potluck, a lot of hot dishes and casseroles, and the only thing that came close to Atkins worthy was one plate of finger sandwiches someone had brought. Britney stocked up on these, pulling them apart so she could roll the ham and turkey inside into little balls, which she then popped into her mouth like they were bonbons. By the time she was done eating, she had built a six-layer-deep wall of bread triangles.

Throughout the meal, it seemed like everyone there found a moment to come over and give condolences. She hardly knew most of these people. They were Ricky's acquaintances, accumulated throughout his seventeen years. It was nice, if a little bit weird, to have stranger after stranger come up and shake her hand, pat her tenderly on the shoulder, and say how sorry they felt for her. "You're the fiancée," they'd typically say. "It's such a tragedy." "I know it's not much of a help, but I'm going to miss him too." She imagined that most of these people must have known Ricky a lot better than she did—they'd known him for years, while she'd only had a few months with him. Still, she was gracious. She smiled demurely and looked the strangers dead in the eye—this seemed to be what they most wanted—while they stretched for a heartfelt connection.

Accepting so much kindness was exhausting. The only relief came when Melissa stopped by. She'd cleaned herself up for the occasion, pulling her curly hair into nice braids, and she'd even put on some mascara and lipstick. Britney had never seen her look so elegant. "How are you holding up?" she asked. The nice thing was that Britney didn't have to answer this question. Melissa knew her so well that a mere shrug explained everything: the shock and confusion, the exhaustion, the numbness, the weirdness of being showered with love from people she'd never met before. Without another word, Melissa positioned herself behind Britney's chair and began kneading the knotted muscles in her shoulders.

Britney's father had demanded that Adam be seated with the family. Up to now, he'd been surprisingly well behaved—Britney figured this was due to the warning her father had given him in the car on their way over—but as soon as Melissa came over, he perked up. In a really obvious way, he started glancing at the two girls. Every five seconds, his eyes would dart back to them and linger in what Britney thought was a leering stare. The only thing that stopped Britney from telling him off was that to do so would mean she had to speak to him. She didn't want to give him any excuse to make a scene.

"Better?" asked Melissa.

"Yeah," said Britney. Squeezing Melissa's hand, she pulled her friend close so she could whisper in her ear. "Listen, I want to say this now because it seems like the right moment and moments like this don't come around too often. You're the only one. The only one in the whole wide world who knows what I'm really like. Whatever happens, I want you to know that."

"Shush," said Melissa. "You don't have to say that. I'm just doing what anyone would do. You know, there's this place in Africa where the society works in this way so that the women are the leaders, and they share all of one another's burdens. When any one member of the community is in pain, the rest of the women rally around her and pick up her slack until she's recovered. I've seen you through worse. I'm not going anywhere."

"See, that's what I mean." Britney squeezed Melissa's hand one more time and then let it go before she could start to cry.

As soon as Melissa had left, Adam leaned over and said,

"Listen, I'm sorry I gave you such a hard time the other night at dinner. I've been thinking about it, and I feel . . . bad. Can we call a truce?"

Britney wasn't sure what to make of this. Knowing Adam, she suspected it might be a trap. She screwed up her face. "I'll think about it," she said.

"Hey, I'll take what I can get," he said.

She could feel someone standing on the other side of her, and with relief, she turned her back to Adam.

The person waiting to talk to her turned out to be a police officer, a leggy, glamorous-looking woman in her mid-twenties. The familiar blue-black uniform looked better on her than Britney remembered it looking on other female cops. It didn't bulk up in the butt like they usually did. The severity of the uniform accentuated her long blond curls. When she squatted on one knee to chat, Britney noticed that her nose was covered in faint freckles, and she was chewing bubble gum.

"I'm Tara Russell," said the woman, "the detective who's looking into Ricky's case. I wanted to take a sec to introduce myself. Listen, can I pull you away for a minute?"

"Um, sure," Britney said.

"Mind if we step outside? I'm dying for a cigarette."

As they walked toward the large double doors at the other end of the room, Detective Russell blew bubbles. Her gum was sour apple green.

Britney was surprised that the detective was so cavalier about smoking on the job. "Are you allowed to do that?" she asked.

The detective frowned. "Why wouldn't I be? We're going outside, aren't we?"

With the windchill, the temperature outside was hitting thirty below, so the two of them stood in the small foyer between the parking lot and the hall. The only thing between them and the elements were some plate glass windows, but these were enough to keep them from shivering.

"You want one?" asked the detective as she pulled a pack of Camel Lights from her purse.

"I'm okay," said Britney.

"If you want one, it's not a problem. It's not like I'm going to tell on you or anything."

"I don't smoke," said Britney. She was nervous, afraid that whatever the detective had to say was going to be more bad news. Why else would they have had to leave the room to talk?

"Well, first, let me see the ring!" Detective Russell's voice, as she said this, swung gleefully.

Tilting her hand back and forth to catch the light and make it twinkle in the diamond, Britney said, "It's only half a carat, but it's got a white gold band. Regular gold is so tacky."

"It's beautiful! Is it inscribed?"

"No." Britney's face fell. She wondered if the fact that the ring wasn't inscribed cheapened it in some way.

"It's a real tragedy the way this happened, isn't it?"

Looking the detective in the eye, Britney saw compassion, but she also saw something else: her eyes had a sharp clarity to them.

"Uh-huh."

"Back when I was in college, I dated a UW football star. He never gave me a ring like that. You should cherish it."

Britney nodded.

Abruptly changing the subject, the detective said, "I know this is an awkward time, but I need to go over some things with you. Right now we're treating this as an accident, so I'm just covering my bases, but—"

Something burst inside Britney. It felt like her veins had turned into waterfalls, the blood rushing, tumbling down toward her stomach. "Have you talked to Digger?" She spoke quickly, the words leaping over each other in a race to the finish.

"Who's Digger?"

"Ricky's hockey buddy. Doug Dietz."

"Well, no. Should I have?"

"I don't know," Britney said. "Probably not. He's been telling people that someone threatened Ricky a few days before he got—passed away. But Digger's the kind of guy who makes things up, you know?"

"Hmm." The detective nodded gravely. "That's interesting." She pulled a thick notepad from her belt and wrote something in it. "I'll tell you what we *have* done. We've performed some forensics on the tire tracks into and out of the gas station, and we've ruled out the possibility that whoever was driving that truck lost control on the ice. There was too much salt on the road. And there wasn't any fishtailing. If he'd lost control, we would have seen signs that he'd tried to brake. But we still haven't ruled out a drunk driver. I mean, he would have had to have been blitzed out of his mind, but in a college town like this, that's not at all inconceivable."

"Do you have any idea who was driving the truck?"

Detective Russell shrugged. She looked around for an ashtray, and not finding one, she stubbed her cigarette out on the sole of her shiny black shoe. "We're running some tests on the paint that scraped off onto Ricky's car," she said, "but I wouldn't hold my breath if I were you. There's not a lot to go on. I mean, a red pickup? Come on, who *doesn't* own one of them?"

"Well . . . What about the Prairie Dogs? They could have done it, right? They were really pissed about what happened at the game. I mean, Digger—"

"I've looked into them already. Most of the team was on the bus headed back to Sun Prairie. The only one who wasn't, Todd Smaltz, and his girlfriend were at the hospital all night."

Britney stiffened. "Then you don't know anything, do you?" She felt like jumping up and down, like pounding her fists against the detective's chest and screaming, "What are you good for if you can't even solve a simple hit and run?" But she didn't. She bounced from foot to foot to help control her adrenaline.

Detective Russell was popping more gum into her mouth. "I'm working on it," she said. "You want to go back inside?" As she said this, the detective adjusted her hair in her reflection in the glass. She touched up her makeup. She seemed totally unaffected by the state she'd put Britney in.

Back inside, just before parting company with Britney, the detective took her by the shoulders and looked her straight in the eyes. "Listen, I want you to know I'm here for you whenever you need me. Here's my private number." She handed Britney a business card. "It doesn't even have to be related to the case. Anything you need, just give me a call. You remind me of what I was like when I was your age."

Britney tried to smile. "Thanks," she said.

"Promise me you'll use it?" the detective said.

"Yeah, okay, I guess," said Britney. "But I hope I don't have to."

eleven

The Computer Rebooter, where Bobby Plumley worked, was more like a shed than an office. The whole place spooked Adam out. It felt like it could easily be the lair of an evil scientist. It was out on the Washington Avenue strip, in a low cluster of windowless buildings not far from the gas station where Ricky had been killed. It had no sign, and instead of a front door, it had a retractable garage door that could only be opened by remote control. Inside, there were computers of all makes and models piled shoulder high in a ring around the messy work area, a long wooden table on which Bobby could play around with seven computers at once. In the darkness along one wall was a row of routers and servers; their red and green lights flickered like the control panels of a spaceship. The only real light came from a fluorescent rod that had somehow been jimmied so it hung loose over the table.

Bobby worked for a guy named Ted Dempsey, but Dempsey was never around, and Bobby ran the show, tearing apart and rebuilding motherboards and towers sometimes until four-thirty in the morning. That is, when he wasn't fiddling with his web site or trying to hack into the Department of Motor Vehicles records. Right now, he and Adam were eating Doritos and playing EverQuest. His T-shirt today showed a drawing of a severed human arm on a plate; underneath, it read Tastes Like Chicken.

Bobby had embedded all sorts of cheats so that his EverQuest character would be unkillable. He explained to Adam that "this means I can go around hacking people up and stealing their money and basically doing whatever I want, and there's nothing they can do about it. They can't even kick me off the game because I've build an override to counteract the host commands."

Adam was pretty handy on a computer himself. He knew all the cheats Bobby was using—they weren't that hard to figure out—but playing an unkillable character was sort of boring. What Adam liked about EverQuest was the web of relationships that you developed throughout the world of the game. You had to think about the consequences of any action you took, and you had to work with the rest of the gaming community to really succeed. If you could just go and slaughter people, what was the point?

It was 10 p.m. and a school night for Adam—not for Bobby because he'd skipped a year and graduated early. Except for last night's dinner in Ricky's honor, it was also his first night off since he'd been hired by Amoeba Records, and there was no way he was going to waste it on doing schoolwork.

"So, you were right," he said, shoving a Dorito into his mouth. "Britney got all weird when I mentioned your name. What did you do to her?"

Bobby's gaze remained on the game. He continued typing commands into the computer throughout their conversation. "What did I do to her? The question is, what did she do to me!"

"Well, tell me."

"It's complicated."

"Everything's complicated. Life is complicated."

"She's just . . ." Bobby paused and frowned at the screen. "She's a messed-up girl." He started tapping the keyboard with a rapid vigor. "Look at that!" He grinned maniacally at Adam. "I just burned that mofo's house down! Let's go see what he's got to steal!"

They played the game for a while—or Bobby played, and Adam watched. Figuring that he wasn't going to get anywhere with his questions, Adam said, "I heard this great CD two days ago at my new job—"

"Oh, man," Bobby cut him off, "I can get you whatever you want for free. I know how to get around all the firewalls. What do you want? Grab a blank CD from the shelf over there. We can burn it right now."

Before they could get the process started, the metal grate that served as a door began rattling. The sound echoed ferociously around the room, bouncing off the concrete floor.

"That must be Melissa," said Bobby. "Can you get it? You just have to push the button against that wall over there."

To reach the automatic door opener, Adam had to watch his feet, picking his way across the room. Spare cords, loose mice, keyboards, and small green plates covered with wires and knobs were strewn everywhere. He actually had to climb over a wall of monitors.

Once the door was open, he discovered it was the same Melissa who was Britney's friend, the redheaded girl who had rubbed her shoulders at the dinner, shivering outside. Well, that's odd, he thought. But he didn't mind her showing up here at all—last night, when she'd been wearing that blue crushed velvet gown, he'd thought she was beautiful, and now, here, even in her ski jacket and woolen cap, nothing had changed.

"Hi, Adam," she said, as if she'd expected to see him, as if they'd known each other all their lives as opposed to having seen each other, what, maybe five times total, and always in passing. They'd never even spoken to each other.

Adam, trying to imagine what her face would look like without her glasses on, had to force himself to stop staring.

"Hi, uh, Melissa."

As Adam pushed the button to shut out the cold and began climbing back over the monitors, Bobby yelled over to the two of them. "Adam was just asking me about Britney. He wants to know what I did to her."

Melissa laughed. "Bobby didn't do anything to Britney. Britney broke *his* heart."

She made it back to the work area before Adam, and sitting down in the metal folding chair he had been using, she said to Bobby, "But that doesn't excuse you from not making it yesterday. What was up? You told me you'd be there."

"I was at the funeral; you just didn't see me."

"Well, you weren't at the reception."

"I wasn't invited."

"When have you ever waited for an invitation?"

Bobby shot her a pained look. He glancing at Adam, who had finally found his way back, and said, "There are more folding chairs over there by the servers."

Adam gazed out into the dark back corner of the room. He could see the folding chairs, but he couldn't see any way to reach them.

Melissa scooted to one side of her chair. When she smiled at him, he noticed she had a dimple on her right cheek. She patted the seat next to her and said, "Don't even try it. You'll kill yourself trying to climb over all that junk. Here. I stole your chair to begin with. Let's share."

God, was she beautiful. Her beauty was embedded in that dimple; it was soaked into the husky edge of her voice; it was deeper than fashion, deeper than skin. Adam found that he was suddenly hoarse. His voice cracked and he blushed as he said,

"I don't think Britney'd be happy to hear about us sharing a chair."

"There are lots of things I do that Britney wouldn't be happy to hear about," she said, winking at him. "So Bobby, do tell. Why weren't you there?"

Bobby glanced skeptically at Adam again, and then he shrugged. If he was trying to be subtle, he was doing a terrible job.

"Oh, don't worry about Adam. He's one of us," said Melissa.

Though he wasn't sure what she meant by this, it felt nice to hear Melissa say it. Since he'd arrived in Madison, he hadn't felt like he belonged, really, anywhere.

Reluctantly, Bobby began to explain. "That funeral sort of freaked me out. I mean . . . Didn't it freak you out?"

"You mean that weird clapping after Britney's speech?"

"No, that was just some lughead asshole. I mean the way Britney was acting. She didn't seem jittery to you?"

"She always seems jittery."

"I don't know, Melissa." Bobby glanced at Adam again. "I thought I saw that look in her eyes."

"What look?"

"*That* look."

"Well, obviously, she had that look again," Melissa said. "She's falling apart. That's why I wish you had been at the reception."

Adam broke in. "What are you guys talking about?"

Melissa turned to Adam. "Sometimes Britney can go to some

pretty dark places. I mean *dark* places. Pitch-black places."

Bobby jumped in to elaborate. "And the harder she tries to act like her life is perfect, the more you can bet that she's breaking apart."

They went on like this for almost an hour, explaining all kinds of things Adam had never noticed: That when she was especially tense, Britney had a way of rapidly, repeatedly cracking her jaw. That she used to hate the hockey thugs and their silly wives as much as Bobby and Melissa did, but after her mother died, she had become obsessed with them and made it her mission to become best friends with them. That her mother's body had never been discovered. The assumption was that it had been pulled into the rapids and smashed on the rocks below Waukesha Falls.

"Jeez," said Adam. "My folks told me she'd been having a hard time, but I had no idea any of this was going on." He felt horrible. If he'd known all this, he would have tried harder to be nice to Britney. He'd been operating under the assumption that she was just a typical popular girl who judged everybody and was always looking for a way to hold on to her feeling of superiority. It felt to Adam now that he was the one who had been refusing to give *her* a chance. He promised himself that he'd show more compassion from here on out.

It was almost eleven-thirty and Mr. Johnson had told Adam to be home by twelve.

"So," he said, "who's going to cart me home? Melissa?"

Without looking up, Bobby said, "Yeah, Melissa, take him home. I've got some serious killing to do here."

"I don't know," she said, winking at him as she grabbed her coat. "I don't think I trust him alone with me."

"Good call," Adam said. "I wouldn't trust me alone with you either."

Once they were outside and headed toward the Johnsons' house, he said, "What I don't understand is, it seems like you two care about Britney a lot. Why does she hate Bobby so much?"

"Bobby? Well, he has his problems too," said Melissa. Abruptly changing the subject, she pushed the play button on her car stereo and said, "Here, listen to this new CD I picked up last week. It's incredible." It was Belle and Sebastian. *Dear Catastrophe Waitress.* "It came out a couple of years ago, but it's great, isn't it?"

"You're kidding, right?"

"You don't like it, do you?" She sounded truly disappointed.

"No, it's not that. It's—I love these guys. I had no idea anybody in this town had ever heard of them."

"Well," she said, "I'm full of surprises."

A prickle of anticipation inched up Adam's back. He hoped he'd have the opportunity to be surprised by her again and again.

They didn't speak much on the ride home, but the music made Adam feel like they were growing more intimate anyway. He almost felt like it would be all right to kiss her when they got to Britney's house, but she got very serious as she pulled into the driveway. He wondered if maybe he'd been imagining the whole thing and if she still thought of him as just that guy who lived in her best friend's house.

"Listen," she said. "You probably shouldn't tell Britney about all the stuff we talked about tonight, okay? I mean, she'd kill me if she knew I still hang out with Bobby."

"Sure," Adam said. He was afraid he looked sort of dumb nodding like this. "No problem."

She winked at him. "See ya."

"Yeah, see ya."

It wasn't until she had driven away that he realized that they had a secret now. They had a secret! And a secret was almost as good as a kiss.

twelve

After the final bell rang on Friday afternoon, Britney hid her head in her locker so she wouldn't have to be confronted again by the pitying looks of her fellow students.

All day she'd been confronted by the eyes of freshman girls, of boys from the school newspaper, of the guys from Hummus, everyone staring, thinking, she was sure, There but for the grace of God go I. She knew that they wanted to impress their sympathy on her, but she wished they would stop staring. If everyone just acted like nothing had happened, maybe she could begin to feel normal again.

When Melissa wandered over, Britney was momentarily disappointed. She'd hoped to hang out with Erin and the other wives, to go somewhere with them and do something mindless, maybe watch TV, while snuggling into their shared memories of Ricky.

"Can I get a ride home?" asked Melissa.

Britney gazed down the hallway. There wasn't a hockey wife within sight. She didn't want to be rude, and she really hadn't spent enough time with Melissa lately, so she said, "Sure."

"I need to stop by the library. Is that okay?"

Britney nodded. Now that she'd committed, she couldn't back out, though hanging around at the library was the last thing she wanted to do.

The two of them made their way across the parking lot toward Britney's VW Bug. Their teeth chattered. Melissa's heavy quilted coat was zipped up to her chin, her scarf wrapped tight, and she could withstand the cold. But Britney was wearing Ricky's letter jacket, and even with the wool roll-top sweater underneath, she could feel the wind crawl in through the buttons. Despite her thick mittens, her fingers were numb.

The ice on the ground was thick and slippery—the girls had to take care with every step not to slip.

"Do you have some time? Let's go to Fresh Grounds and grab a latte," said Melissa. "I've got something I want to talk to you about."

"Oh? What's that?"

They didn't look at each other as they spoke. It was so cold out that despite their coats, their muscles contracted and stiffened—any extra movement was another opportunity to expose some new bit of skin to the bracing wind.

"There's this, um—oh, now I'm embarrassed—this boy I like."

Britney spun on her and clasped her hands. "A boy! You mean like a real live boy? Of the human persuasion?"

"Don't make fun of me."

"Melissa, this is great. Look at you! You're blushing!"

As they neared the car, Britney fumbled with her keys. Pressing the unlock button was hard to do with frozen fingers. While she fumbled, Melissa pulled her door open. Britney thought it was odd that the doors were already unlocked.

"I could swear I locked my car this morning."

"Sometimes when it's cold, you think you've locked it when you really haven't."

"No. I know I locked it. I distinctly remember hearing the chime and thinking about this car we had when I was little that used to say 'a door is ajar' every time I got in."

"So," said Melissa, changing the subject. "The thing is, you know him."

"God, tell me already! I'm so excited!"

"Let's get warm first."

The two of them climbed into their respective sides of the car. As Britney settled into the driver's seat, she heard something crunch underneath her. After fishing around for a moment, she pulled out a cracked jewel case. Under the clear plastic glimmered a blank CD. Someone had scrawled the words WITH LOVE on it in large block letters.

She froze up.

"Look at this," she said, handing the CD to Melissa. "This is . . ." She shuddered involuntarily.

As Melissa studied the CD, Britney put her key in the ignition.

"Hurry up and turn the heat on," she said. "It's freezing in here!"

Melissa's attitude annoyed Britney. One of the things she liked best about her friend was that she could always be relied on to put aside whatever she was thinking about to focus on the melodrama of Britney's life. "You don't seem too concerned," she said.

"I want to tell you about this boy."

"Whatever. I'm a little freaked out right now, Melissa."

As soon as she'd opened the door, Britney had begun to feel incredibly anxious. It was as if she'd known, even before finding the CD, that her space had been invaded—as if someone had come in while she was in class and rubbed their greasy palms all over her stuff, not taking anything, but leaving a nasty scent behind.

In silence, Britney turned on the engine and flicked the heat up to high.

"Well, let's hear what's on it," said Melissa with a little sigh that Britney took as a subtle criticism. She popped the CD into the stereo, and the two of them waited for what would come next.

From the very first notes, a chill crept down Britney's back. The song began with soft finger picking on what sounded like an acoustic guitar. It had an almost Celtic air to it, the mystical far-off quality of a mythic dirge. She recognized it immediately.

Her fingers tensed on the steering wheel. Her stare drove into the windshield. Then the lyrics began. . . .

> There's a lady who's sure
> all that glitters is gold
> and she's buying a stairway to heaven. . .

After a few verses, the song began to change. Static overtook the melody, as though the song was coming from a radio station that was on the verge of breaking up. The static grew louder and more disturbing as the CD played on—now it sounded like machine-gun fire, a rapid assault of feedback.

Melissa gasped. "I think someone's saying something. Is that a voice?"

Listening closely, Britney could heard it. A murmuring, threatening gurgle of sound that when she concentrated, she could make out as words.

"*. . . deserved everything he got, and you know it. I only wish I could have stuck around to see him writhe in pain. . . . When I come for you, I promise, I'll make sure I watch every minute of it. . . .*"

Britney shrieked at the top of her lungs. It was like she was hyperventilating. She suddenly felt so hot, no, so cold, no, so hot. She tore at her letter jacket, but in her frenzy, she couldn't get the thing off. Somewhere—it felt like very far away—she could hear Melissa screaming too. She could feel Melissa's hand on her shoulder; it felt like a tentacle, a slimy, twisty thing reaching to throttle her. She screamed louder, harder. "Turn it off! Turn it off!" But the words weren't coming out right, and the horrible white noise played on and on.

Finally she couldn't scream any longer and she collapsed onto the steering wheel, sobbing.

Melissa stopped the CD.

Neither of them spoke for a long, long time.

When Melissa did finally speak, she did so in even, soft tones. "Are you okay?"

"Do I look okay?" Britney shouted between sobs. She cried for she didn't know how long. "How did they know about 'Stairway to Heaven'? That was our song. Mine. And Ricky's. I mean, nobody knew about it except me and Ricky. It . . . We . . . It . . . And the way the guy was talking . . ."

"Someone's been spying on you, obviously." Melissa voice was soothing—in times of crisis, she was the best person to have around. She could be both firm and tender all at once. "We need to—"

A snowball exploded on the windshield, and the girls both screamed again.

Then, from nowhere, Adam was racing toward them, mounds of snow in both hands. He threw himself onto the hood of the car and rubbed the snow in like an overeager window washer. He grinned maniacally.

It was all too overwhelming for Britney. Melissa leapt from the car to confront Adam and Britney leaned her head on the steering wheel and let the sobs wash through her.

She couldn't hear what they were saying, but when she finally felt calm enough to look up, Britney saw that they were both smiling. There was a sassiness to Melissa's body language that Britney had never seen before. She dully registered that Adam must be Melissa's secret crush. They kept glancing over at Britney in the car, and if she didn't know Adam so well, she would have sworn that the expression on his face was one of concern.

Jumping back into the car, Melissa spoke curtly. "We have to call that detective what's-her-name immediately. We have to tell her about this. Here. Do you have that card she gave you? I'll do it."

"No." Britney struggled to hold herself together. "I don't have it. I don't want to talk to her. I want my dad. I want to talk to my dad."

Melissa thought about this for a moment. "Okay," she said. "Come on, scoot over. I'll drive."

Riding off toward her father's office in the passenger seat of her own car, Britney felt like her insides had been scraped out. Even though nothing had been stolen, she felt like she'd lost something, like she wasn't safe anywhere, not even in her own skin.

thirteen

Mr. Johnson was in consultation with a client. Closed into his office, behind a thick oak door. Melissa tried to explain to his assistant, Tamara, that this was an emergency—as if it wasn't already obvious from the rivulets of black tears running down Britney's cheeks. She stood there, hunched over Tamara's desk, which, for someone whose sole job was to keep the office organized and make sure that anything Mr. Johnson needed was easy to find, was a disaster. Folders and documents binder-clipped together were piled everywhere, stained with coffee rings and dark splotches of soy sauce; the folders even spilled onto the floor.

"I don't know," Tamara kept saying. "I'm not supposed to disturb him when he's with a client."

"It's an emergency!" said Melissa again. She was doing most of the talking. It was all Britney could do to sit silently, trying to hold herself together, on the antique couch, a deep royal blue with wooden scrollwork on the arms that her mother had purchased when she worked at the office.

Suddenly Britney ran to the desk and, knocking over a mug of pens and spilling Tamara's bottle of water, she yanked the phone away and shouted into it. "Dad? I need to talk to you! Tamara won't let us in!"

Then she very calmly placed the phone back in its cradle and returned to her perch on the couch. Acting like there had been no scene at all, as if she were just hanging out here, not even upset, Britney crossed her legs and waited. To make her point even more obvious, she casually picked up one of the old *Newsweek*s that lay on the art deco coffee table and began to leaf through it.

"He won't come out," said Tamara as she tried to clean the water off the documents strewn around her desk. Picking them up in big bundles, she flicked the water into her trash can. Britney hoped that some of them were important; it would serve Tamara right if they got ruined.

It took Britney's father a few minutes, but sure enough, the door to his office slipped open a crack and he came out, shutting it quickly behind him to protect his client's privacy. Britney was overjoyed to see him. He had that familiar hangdog droop to his shoulders—a defeated shuffle to his gait that had arrived soon after Britney's mother died and never left. When he looked at her with those tender, pained eyes, she felt so safe that her whole body quivered.

Tamara shot Melissa a dirty look, but she didn't say anything. She acted like she'd known Mr. Johnson would come talk to the girls all along. Anyway, she was too busy shutting down the spider solitaire game on her computer to cause any more trouble.

"Tamara," said Mr. Johnson, "would it be okay if—" He glanced at the girls with a look that said to her, I'm sorry to get in your way, but if you could just give us a moment or two alone?

"Sure. Okay," Tamara said. "I want a muffin anyway." Then, putting on the sickliest saccharine voice Britney'd ever heard, she said, "Can I get you anything?"

He just shook his head wearily.

Britney was so overcome that she just sat there with her head in her lap while Melissa explained about the CD and the scene in the car. Throughout the conversation, Mr. Johnson rubbed Britney's back with the palm of one hand. He listened gravely, seriously considering every word Melissa said.

"Oh, Brit, I'm so sorry," he said once Melissa had finished. "You must have felt like the world was ending."

Britney nodded.

"Do you have the CD?" he asked.

Melissa handed it over, and he frowned, studying it carefully.

"I think we need to tell Detective Russell about this." He glanced at Britney and, seeing how torn up she was, said, "It's okay. I'll do it. I suspect it's just a prank—probably those hockey guys. I can't count how many times I've seen them in court over idiotic behavior like this." He took Britney's hand between his two palms. "I'll see what I can do, though, okay, sweetie? Detective Russell and I will get this sorted out. In the meantime, do you still have those bath salts from The Body Shop that Grandma Johnson sent you for Christmas?"

Britney shrugged. It was as much of a response as she could muster.

"When your mother was especially rattled about things, she used to take a long bath to calm herself down. Maybe you should try it. Those salts are supposed to be therapeutic. They've got aromatherapy in them or something. Or you could— here, I'll give you some cash. Pamper yourself. Whatever you think might relax you."

"I've got an idea. Why don't you roll up a giant-size joint and get baked out of your skull? It always helps me forget all the bullshit."

The three of them—Britney, her father, and Melissa—all looked toward this new voice. There, leaning against the inner-office doorjamb, stood a gaunt, rangy guy in his early twenties. He was wearing a tattered black leather jacket over a Megadeth T-shirt. Looped through his dirty blue jeans was a thick black belt; the buckle was huge and brass: a screaming eagle flying out of an American flag. His curly red hair looked like it hadn't been washed in weeks.

Before anyone could say anything, the guy raised his hands as though to calm them down. "Joke. It's a joke," he said.

"Karl?" The look on Melissa's face was one of abject shock.

"Karl, what—why—don't tell me you got arrested again!"

Smiling wryly, Karl said, "Ed here's helping me hook up a job."

Karl was Melissa's brother. He'd been caught working at a crystal meth lab a couple of years ago—just a few months after Britney's mother had died—and shipped off to prison in Waupun. The lab hadn't been his operation. His job had been to drive the chemicals and formaldehyde in from the feed store out in North Bristol. With Mr. Johnson as his lawyer, he'd been sentenced to five years. The other guys all got twenty.

Britney had known Karl since they were kids. When she'd been a real small child, she'd seen him lingering around Melissa's house whenever she came over to play. Then, as the girls got older, he was there less and less. At sixteen, he dropped out of high school, and this was such a blow to Melissa's college professor parents that they kicked him out of the house. Before he'd been sent off to jail, Britney and Melissa used to hang around with him on State Street.

He winked at Britney. "Hey, cutie," he said. "Nice letter jacket. I didn't know you played on the hockey team."

Melissa turned skeptically to Mr. Johnson. "You got him a job?"

"He starts tomorrow," said Mr. Johnson.

"Doing what?"

"Why don't you ask him?" There was a fatherly glow of pride in Mr. Johnson's face.

"You know, that meat-packing factory," Karl said.

"The Bavarian Brat Haus," Mr. Johnson interjected.

"Yeah, that place."

Melissa rolled her eyes.

Britney and Melissa had had many long talks about how sad she got when she thought about her brother's troubled life. Her biggest fear in the world was that he'd never get his life together.

"Karl—" Mr. Johnson said sharply, nodding toward the inner office.

"I just wanted to see if everything was all right."

"Well, it is."

"So-or-ry," Karl said, chuckling. "Britney, it's always a pleasure." He winked at her again. "And Melissa . . ." His voice trailed off. He shrugged as if he couldn't think of anything worth saying to her and shut himself back in the office.

"Okay, kiddo," Mr. Johnson said when they were alone again. "I don't want you to worry about this stuff with that CD. I'm going to take care of it. I'll never let anyone hurt you." He stood up and coaxed her toward him. "Come on, now, give me a hug."

There were his arms around her again, holding her so tight she almost believed, at least for a moment, that he could protect her from anything.

"Better?" he said.

She tried to smile. "A little bit," she lied.

fourteen

That night while Britney was taking her bath, Adam slipped out of the house through the garage door that opened off the corridor holding the washer and dryer. He squeezed between Britney's car and the junk piled against the wall, past the riding lawn mower and the huge lidded garbage can, past the cardboard boxes piled high with Christmas decorations, past the snowblower and the stacked sawhorses. As he made his way around Britney's snowboard, he inadvertently kicked her father's skis, sending them flopping down on the front wheel hub of her Bug. He hoped that he hadn't damaged anything, but it was hard to tell in the darkness of the garage, and he couldn't turn on the light because he didn't want anyone to catch him out here.

Wrapping his duck-hunting jacket tight around him and adjusting the plaid scarf around his neck, he stepped out the door at the back of the garage and onto the hard-packed snow covering the backyard.

The wind hissed off the snowdrifts. It bit into his cheeks and prickled at his fingertips, but he was willing to put up with this at the moment. His need for a cigarette was that strong. Turning his back to the wind so he could create a cove to shield the flame, he lit up and breathed the smoke deep into his lungs.

Adam had started smoking during the tumultuous period last year when he had started doing most everything he now regretted.

He'd made a lot of mistakes during his final few months in New Hampshire: the failing grades, the recklessly driving through people's backyards, which had garnered him a suspended license. He'd begun to hang out with rich kids guys like Fisher and Hal, smoking their pot and pretending they had something in common. He knew that they were allowed to mess up in ways that he wasn't—their fathers had the pull to cover for them, and even if they failed every single one of their classes, they'd still get into the best Ivy League schools. He didn't even like those guys. But he knew that by buddying up to them, he'd enrage his parents, and that had been his only goal at the time. He was so hurt by the fact that their marriage was falling apart that he felt he had to hurt them back in any way he could.

Being shipped to Madison had come almost as a relief. Nobody here knew how much trouble he'd gotten himself into back home.

Once the wind calmed down, the cold wasn't so bad. Gazing back at the house, he smiled. A single window on the second floor was casting light out into the frigid air. Something about that one lonely light made him feel less lonely himself. This wasn't so bad, living here with the Johnsons. Especially if it meant getting to know Britney's friend Melissa better.

He knew the light must be coming from the bathroom where Britney was soaking in the tub. She'd been in a bad mood all night—not that he blamed her. From what Melissa had told him, that CD had been pretty freaky.

He stared up at the house for a while, feeling sentimental. The roof was tiered into multiple levels, and his eyes roamed over it, mapping the smooth flow of snow there.

On the roof of the garage, there was a large dark lump of something. Adam couldn't tell what it was. It looked like a trash bag. He wondered how it had gotten up there.

Then he saw it move.

He froze and watched it closely.

It moved again.

Now he could make out the contours. Someone was crouching up there. He could make out the head under a dark black stocking cap. There was the torso. Whoever it was up there was staring into the bathroom window, spying on Britney while she took her bath.

As stealthily as he could, he reached down and picked up a clump of snow, which he mashed into a snowball.

One. Two. Three.

He threw the snowball with all his might, but he missed. When the snowball splattered on the garage roof, the guy turned to see where it had come from. He spied Adam and bolted over the other side.

Adam chased around to the front of the house. Just as he got there, he saw a chubby figure in a black snowmobile suit fall into the snow and then scramble to his feet and break into a run.

Adam ran after him. Well, he sort of ran. The snow was so deep that it was impossible to move with any real speed.

The figure made it to the road and broke into a sprint toward the Montgomerys' driveway, sticking to the plowed pavement, where it was easier to run. He had a pretty good lead by the time Adam broke through the drifts.

Speeding after him, Adam almost cornered him under the basketball hoop, but with a dart, the guy shifted directions, sending Adam slipping to his knees, then took off again back toward the main street.

The two of them trudged down the middle of the road. Adam was lighter and more athletic. He gradually gained ground on the guy until finally, just as they reached the corner where the cul-de-sac hooked up with Maple Run Road, he tackled him.

They wrestled for a minute, Adam struggling to pin the guy to the ground, the guy twisting and kicking to get away. When Adam got the guy on his back, he raised his fist to punch him in the jaw. Then he looked at the guy's face finally, and he was shocked to discover it was Bobby Plumley.

"Bobby? You freak. What's the matter with you?"

"Nothing. What's the matter with *you*?" Bobby responded.

"You perv. What the hell do you think you were doing up there?"

"I wasn't doing anything."

"I saw you."

"I don't care what you saw. It's not what you think." Bobby looked scared.

"Oh?" Adam sat back into the snow. He knew that if Bobby tried to run again, he'd catch him. "You were spying on Britney. You were fucking peeping on her in the bathroom. Did you catch her naked? Jesus. Maybe she was right about you after all."

"You don't understand."

"What? What don't I understand? You know? You're lucky I didn't go grab one of Mr. Johnson's guns and shoot you with it."

Bobby stood up and dusted off his snowmobile suit. He rubbed his back where Adam had barreled into him. "Okay, look," he said, sitting down on the snowdrift next to Adam. "Maybe I did see Britney naked just now, but that's not why I'm out here tonight. I can get porn off the internet if I want to see naked girls, okay?"

Adam listened skeptically. "Then why are you here?"

"Remember all the stuff Melissa and I told you about the other night? What we didn't say was that Britney is bonkers. She and I used to talk, okay? We used to be really, really close."

"That doesn't—"

Bobby rolled on. "Did you know that her mother was a

schizophrenic? No? I didn't think so. Did you know she thinks that her mother's death wasn't an accident? I don't think you knew that either. And I bet you didn't know that she thinks she was responsible for her mother's death."

"I don't—"

"But she does. She thinks someone was after her, that whoever killed her mother had actually been trying to get to her. You didn't know that. You don't know anything. But I do, so why don't you leave me alone?"

Something about Bobby's story sounded fishy to Adam. It was all so *complicated*. Wasn't the simplest answer usually the right one? Didn't it just make a whole lot more sense if Bobby, who Adam knew was in love with Britney, was stalking her?

"You know what, Bobby? None of that has anything to do with you sitting on the roof of the garage and peeking in the bathroom window. Come on. Tell me the truth. Or do you want me to get Britney and you can tell her?"

The look of horror that spread across Bobby's face was proof enough to Adam that he was right.

"No. Don't do that. Please, please don't do that."

"Oh, don't beg, Bobby. It makes you look even more pathetic than you already are."

"I thought we were friends."

"Yeah, well, that's before I caught you peeping through the window at my real friend, Britney." Hearing himself say this, he was shocked and surprised, but he knew it was true: Britney *was* his real friend.

"I wasn't peeping!"

"Yeah, right."

Bobby curled his arms over his knees and crossed them in front of his face. He stared coldly out into the distance. "You don't get it at all," he said icily. "I don't want her to get hurt. I'm trying to protect her."

The way Bobby said this, with such gravity, such conviction, almost convinced Adam that he believed it.

"You're protecting her from what?"

Bobby's bottom lip curled into a frown. He seemed to be struggling with some dark urge inside himself. "From herself," he said. "Just forget it, okay? There's no way you'd understand."

Adam had had enough of this. He stood up. The wind was picking up again, and he shoved his hands into the inner pockets of his coat to keep his fingers warm.

"Go home, Bobby," he said.

Without looking back, he began to walk toward the house.

"Wait," Bobby called after him. "You're not going to tell her, are you?"

Adam ignored him and kept walking. He wasn't sure if he'd tell Britney or not, but he figured it was best to keep Bobby scared. For a while at least.

fifteen

This was unheard of: the mighty Rabid Raccoons, the unde-
feated state champs, usually so vicious, so pitiless and awesome,
were playing as though they'd just learned how to skate. Their
shots were wild, nowhere near the goal. Their passes were slow
and obvious—easy to pick off. Their defense just wasn't there.
On the day when they should have come storming onto the ice,
full of unquenchable bloodlust, focused like cruise missiles on
showing the world that Ricky's death had not been in vain,
they were playing like they had no heart at all.

The Portage Possums, the worst team in the league—their
record was the mirror opposite of the Raccoons'—had scored
first and second and third. Now they were into the final period,
and the Raccoons still hadn't retaliated.

The fans had grown restless and angry. Deafening boos and

shouts of "You guys suck!" circled the rink like thunder. During a time-out near the end of the second period, someone had thrown a Big Gulp of Pepsi over the glass at Digger; it missed him, but the brown liquid had splattered everywhere.

In the front row, the hockey wives huddled together, their shoulders slumped, glum expressions on their faces. They were in shock. Erin had roused them into leading a few cheers early in the game, but as the clock clicked forward, they found inspiration harder and harder to come by. Now they watched morosely, elbows on knees, frowning faces embedded deep in their fists, as their men threw their pride away.

Britney felt like it was all her fault. If she had just kept Ricky with her for five more minutes that night—even if it had meant five more minutes of fighting—he wouldn't have been at that gas station at that precise instant. All of history would have been altered.

As she sat there brooding, she obsessively fingered the hockey pin on Ricky's letter jacket. Except for the funeral, she'd worn the jacket every day since his death. Like a badge of fidelity.

Cindy said, "To think I turned down the Tomlinsons for this. They pay fifteen dollars an hour, and their baby just lies there and sleeps. I could have watched *American Idol* and walked away with forty-five bucks tonight."

Usually someone would have responded to this. Jodi would have said, "Yeah, but you'd have to change diapers. You'd have to touch nasty baby butt." Or Erin would have told her that she should have taken the job anyway. "What you should have done is wait there until the Tomlinsons were off to dinner and then pack the baby up and bring him here with you." But they were all too unhappy for this kind of patter.

Britney was worried about her place in the group. Now that Ricky was gone, she feared the other girls might gradually distance themselves from her. They'd all been friends forever, since freshman year at least, and she knew from experience—from all those times before she'd been accepted when Erin had seen her in the halls and called out to her mockingly, "Hey, I *love* your blouse. Where'd you get it? Wal-Mart?"—how cruel they could be if they wanted to.

"Well, it looks like Troy's not getting any perks tonight," Erin said as she munched on a stale nacho coated in liquid cheese.

The other girls nodded sagely.

Erin could turn on people so quickly, and since she was without question the leader, if she decided Britney was no longer worthy, the other girls would all follow suit.

She'd have to go back to sitting at the games with her father and Melissa. She loved them both, and sitting with them wouldn't be that horrible, except now all Melissa wanted to do was talk to Adam, and Britney didn't think she could tolerate that. Earlier in the game, when it still looked like the Raccoons had a chance, she'd popped up to say hi, and Melissa—who was making herself more attractive by the day, styling her hair and wearing more and more fashionable clothes—had been so engrossed in Adam's inane chatter about "the best album ever" that she barely acknowledged Britney's presence.

"Hey, everybody," she said, trying to pull the hockey wives into a huddle. "Don't you think we should make some noise? Let the guys know we're still behind them?" The shrugs and signs that greeted this idea were just about what she'd expected. "Well, if nobody else will, I'll do it."

"You can do what you want," said Daphney, "but it's not going to help. I just hope this game doesn't ruin the party."

"Oh, it'll ruin the party," said Erin. "You can count on that."

Britney was sick of this. She was sick of everything.

Jumping to her feet, she began to shout. "Come on, Raccoons, show us what you're made of." Her voice was strong and when she raised it, it climbed up the register. It pierced the silence of the stands. She could feel people turning to look at her, but nobody was joining in yet.

The wives all had their heads in their hands. Well, if they're too embarrassed to support their boyfriends, thought Britney, that's their problem. I'm going to make sure the guys know I appreciate them.

"Do it for Ricky!" she shouted. She liked the sound of that. She liked the idea that anyone who looked would see her, in Ricky's oversized letter jacket, shouting his name. She said it again.

"Do it for Ricky."

Digger, who was on the team bench just across the glass from Britney, craned his thick neck to look back at her. Everything about him was big, but still, he had an especially large mouth, which naturally turned down at the corners.

When he'd been younger, the upperclassmen called him Fish Face, but now there was no one left who could beat him up. When he did grin, his face was all teeth. He was grinning now. He raised a clenched fist in Britney's direction, a show of unity and strength. Then he started chanting with her.

"Do it for Ricky."

Seeing Digger chant, Cindy joined in. She didn't want him to think she didn't care. She was a big girl, tall and wide-hipped, and though most people saw her as one of the cutest girls in school, she'd confided in Britney once that she believed Digger, with his beefy thuggish looks, was the best she'd ever be able to do for herself. She was jumpy when he was around, always trying to do whatever she thought he might think she should be doing.

"Do it for Ricky."

A few more people joined in with each recitation.

"Do it for Ricky."

And the team began to play with more vigor. They got meaner. They bodychecked. They looked for one another on the pass and set up for face-offs like they actually cared. Within a minute, they'd scored their first goal.

The stands erupted. Everyone was chanting now. Clapping. Hooting and hollering.

As the chant made its way around the rink, it gradually morphed. Britney almost couldn't believe what she was hearing.

"Do it for Britney. Do it for Britney."

They stomped their feet in rhythm with the chant, and so

many people had joined in that the stands vibrated like they were going to collapse.

When Digger was put back into the game, he immediately elbowed one of the Possums' forwards in the jaw. The refs didn't see it, but they saw the Possum retaliate, grabbing Digger by the neck and punching at his face. Digger was a whole lot bigger than the guy; he just shrugged him off. He could have beaten the guy to a bloody pulp, but he'd already gotten what he was after. The guy was thrown in the penalty box, and the Raccoons had a one-man advantage. They capitalized five seconds later, getting their second goal.

From then on out, they had the Possums on the run. The tide had turned. Final score: 4–3, Raccoons.

As they skated off the ice, each Raccoon in turn pointed a finger in Britney's direction.

"Well, Britney," Erin said, a little wryly, "you're getting big props tonight."

Britney beamed.

For the first time since Ricky died, she felt almost normal again.

Almost.

Just as everyone was getting up to leave, an explosion of gunshots filled the air. They echoed off the walls and, a second later, one of the two scoreboards hanging at either end of the rink exploded in sparks.

There was utter chaos. Everyone screaming. Rushing for the exits. Standing on tiptoes in search of the shooter. Bodies pressed and pushing up against bodies in a jumble by the doors.

Britney thought she saw Detective Russell, blond hair flying at her back as she ran in the opposite direction, toward the place where the shots seemed to have come from.

The hockey wives clung to one another's coats, huddled together in hopes of feeling safer. Jodi and Daphney were crying. Erin kept repeating, "I can't believe this. I can't believe this. I can't believe this." Britney held tight to them.

She knew those shots had been meant for her. As she and the other hockey wives ran across the parking lot toward Erin's SUV, she had the feeling that someone was watching her, waiting for the opportunity to get her alone, and then . . .

It sent chills down her back just thinking about it.

Twice she heard footsteps running toward her back, and both times she spun around to find no one there.

When small groups of people moved past her, she thought she heard them whispering her name. She couldn't tell if this was her imagination or if it was real. She kept thinking she heard them say things like, "Not now . . . but soon."

sixteen

"Have you made up your mind yet?" asked Adam.

Britney was watching TV—or trying to watch. She'd been conscious of him staring at her for a while, and no matter how hard she tried to ignore him, she couldn't—he was worse than a fly buzzing around her head.

"About what?"

"Our truce."

In everything that had happened since then, she'd almost forgotten all about this truce of his. She glanced at him skeptically to let him know she was hearing him, but she didn't say anything.

"I mean, it's been like four days. How long does it take for you to make up your mind?"

He looked like he hadn't washed his hair in three days. It

hung in limp, spooky spikes toward his eyes, making him look a vampire.

"I don't know, Adam. I've been really freaked out, you know?"

"So you haven't even thought about it."

He nodded in an I-told-you-so way, as though he'd proved something to himself about her.

She turned back to the TV. It was Sunday night. *Alias* was on. Her favorite show. But she couldn't concentrate.

"Look," he said. "I know I can be a dick, okay?"

He scooted to the edge of the chair he was sitting in and playfully boxed at the air around her head.

"Don't you dare touch me," she said.

"I'm just messing around."

He had the most mischievous grin she'd ever seen. She hated to admit this, but it was charming. It was harder to remain annoyed with him when he grinned like that. She wished he'd stop.

"If you're trying to get on my good side because you've got a crush on Melissa, it's not going to work," she said.

"Who said I've got a crush on Melissa?"

She threw a pillow at him. "See, that's why you're so frustrating," she said. "Can't you give a straight answer to anything?"

There was that smile again. "Maybe I've got a crush on you."

"God help me."

"You're blushing," he said.

She touched her face and scowled at him. Then she went

back to watching her TV show. There was some sort of chase going on in Siberia, but she'd missed so much of the story by now that she had no idea why.

"What do you want to know? I'll give you a straight answer."

"Do you have a crush on Melissa?"

"Ask me a different question. Anything but that."

"What did you do to get shipped out here?" Britney asked.

He tapped his lower lip in an exaggerated show of how hard he was thinking. "My parents just thought it would be better for me to be away for a while."

"But I know you did something. My dad told me you'd gotten in some sort of trouble."

"It was just stupid stuff. Smoking pot and things like that."

"See, you're lying," she said.

"Okay, you want to know the truth?" His whole demeanor had changed. He usually flayed himself out in a lazy way, arms and legs everywhere, but now he seemed to shrink, to pull inward. "I got kicked out of school."

"For something bad?"

He nodded gravely. He seemed to be actually telling the truth. It sent a chill down her spine.

Then that grin popped back onto his face. "I'm *crazy loco*," he said in a gurgling, mock-scary voice. He crossed his eyes and puffed out his cheeks. "And I'm coming for you next. What will it be? The tickle attack or the nudgie?" He rolled the tips of his fingers together as though he were scheming nefariously.

Britney tried to remain unamused, but she couldn't stop the grin from breaking across her face.

She laughed. They both laughed.

"God," she said, squeezing the tears away. "That's the first time I think I've laughed since Ricky died."

"So, truce?" Adam said, holding his hand out for her to shake.

"No," she said, and snapped back to attention over the TV. Maybe she was going to forgive him—in fact, she was sure of it—but it seemed only fair to tease him a little since that's what she knew he would do in her shoes.

"Fine," said Adam, "but I'm going to operate as if you said yes. I already have been, actually. You're not going to believe me, but the other night I protected you from an intruder."

"What are you talking about?"

"I caught someone spying on you. Right out back there."

"Who? When?" She felt like someone had just wrestled a plastic bag over her head.

"On Friday. While you were taking that bath."

"But who was it?"

She was sweating suddenly. If there was one place she thought she was safe, it was here at home.

"I shouldn't tell you. You're going to say, 'I told you so.'"

"It was Bobby, wasn't it? Bobby Plumley was spying on me!"

"Don't worry about it, though. I chased him away and told him I'd kick his ass if I ever caught him over here again."

Bobby Plumley! That freak of nature.

For all she knew, he might be watching her right this second. She had to get out of here. She had to go somewhere where she could think. There was only one place. The Sanctuary. She hadn't been there in months—not since she first started dating Ricky—but she was sure it would still have the calming power it always used to have over her. There was something special about that patch of earth, like someone or something protected it.

As she ran out the door, she could hear Adam shouting after her, "Hey, where are you going? I didn't mean to . . . Don't be . . . Jesus, I've pissed you off again, haven't I?"

She didn't have time for his noise right now, though. If she didn't get out of the house right this instant, she was sure she would pass out.

seventeen

There she was.

He'd parked down the hill around a bend in the road, and it took him a few minutes to make his way back, but now he'd found her.

As Britney wandered up the path that led to the lake, trudging through the snow, he'd kept to the woods. She couldn't see him, but he could see her. His view was blocked a bit by the trees from this vantage, but he didn't want to get much closer.

Knowing where she was and what she was doing was enough. All he needed for his purposes. Surprise was his best friend. Stay hidden. Stay stealthy. As long as he kept his ski mask on, no one would be able to recognize him.

She sat down on a park bench and gazed out toward the

lake. What was she looking for? All that was out there at this time of year were ice-fishing shacks.

And she wasn't dressed for the weather. No hat. No scarf. No gloves. Her only protection from the elements was the letter jacket she always wore nowadays. He was bundled up in a snowmobile suit, and he still felt the chill. How could she stand it?

Watch a while longer, he told himself. See what she does.

He heard an engine purring behind him, the crunch of ice and snow under tires. If he peered, he could just make out the parking lot. The rear bumper of Britney's yellow Bug. Darkness. Then a splotch of red rolled into view.

Scampering back toward the parking lot, he hid behind a pine tree and peered into the clearing. What he saw was a red pickup truck. A Ford Ranger—similar to the one he himself owned, except his was cooler, decked out with designer hubs and a killer sound system. The truck must be at least ten years old; rust had spread across the wheel wells and formed little sores all over the hood. The person who hopped out of it was tall. His features were shrouded behind the deep fur-lined hood of his parka. He walked like he knew where he was going.

He ran back to his post in the woods and saw that Britney was right where he'd left her. He crouched. He waited.

A few moments later, he spotted the tall guy again. He got a better look this time—blue jeans, a black, thigh-length parka. Who was this guy, and what was he doing here?

More important, how strong was this guy? It was hard to

tell from the parka he was wearing. Strong enough to put up a fight?

The paths through Menominee Park wound around and cut across one another; only one led directly toward the clearing by the lake. The guy was walking down one of the smaller ones. He'd found a long broken tree limb and was using it as a walking stick. The guy turned at the fork and walked right past him, so close that he curled up and pressed himself into a bush, shutting his eyes tight, as though this would help shield him. He stayed this way for a minute or two.

Then the guy started moving toward Britney. She had her back to him, and he was walking quietly. When he was just a few feet behind her, he stopped. He gazed out at the lake. She still didn't see him.

Tense, on his feet now, he was ready to pounce.

Suddenly the two of them—Britney and the guy—were talking. He couldn't hear what they were saying, but from their body language, they seemed to be exchanging friendly words. Or maybe not. Britney half turned on the bench while she spoke. She seemed guarded, her head and shoulders angled away from the guy—could she tell there was someone else watching them? And the guy kept fiddling with his stick, as though contemplating the correct moment to turn it into a weapon.

They were arguing. Then the guy broke into a rueful laugh.

Get the guy first, then deal with Britney. If he acted fast, the guy would never know what hit him.

He jumped from his hiding place and ran through the snow, stumbling over hidden roots and shrubs. He leapt, threw a diving fist at the guy, but he missed and landed sprawling in the snow.

Then the guy was on top of him—swinging hard. Blows hit his stomach, his arms, his face. The guy yanked off his mask. He was exposed.

He could hear the guy swearing at him, calling him crazy. Britney was shouting at both of them, hysterical. "Stop!" she said. "Stop it. Karl, get out of here!"

By the time he was back on his feet, the guy had run off.

Britney was still there, though, standing a few feet away, her arms crossed. She was staring at him.

"Bobby!" she said, the rage in her voice barely under control.

"Where'd he go?" Bobby asked, looking around in a frenzy.

"How am I supposed to know?" Her eyes were burning. She was full of spite.

Bobby brushed the snow off his snowmobile suit. In the distance, he could hear the truck starting up and peeling away.

"Well, are you all right?"

He reached out to touch her on the elbow, but she pulled violently back.

"Don't touch me! I swear to God, Bobby, I'm going to have you arrested!" she said.

Holding his hands up in surrender, he said, "That guy was going to attack you. I could feel it."

Britney said nothing in response. What looked like a mixture of rage and fear and disgust swirled around on her face. Her gaze lingered on Bobby for a second longer, then she shuddered—or was she just shivering from the cold? She picked something—he couldn't tell what it was—out of the snow at her feet and turned her back on him.

He shouted after her. "Wait! Aren't you even going to say thank you?"

Alone again, he tried to remember if he knew anybody named Karl. There was only one person he could think of. Melissa's dirtbag brother. He'd always known that guy was trouble.

eighteen

Britney sipped her peppermint tea. Her toes bounced rapidly inside her thermal-lined snow boots. She was clicking her jaw back and forth, back and forth. She had fished an *Entertainment Weekly* out of the magazine rack that Fresh Grounds provided for its customers, but she gave up on it quickly. She couldn't concentrate.

She was still shaken up. As though to gauge the changing state of her emotions, she held her hand up in front of her and tried to control the shaking. She couldn't.

It was almost nine-thirty, and Detective Russell still hadn't arrived.

Nine thirty-five. Fresh Grounds was going to close at ten.

Britney was about ready to give up and head home, but just then the detective walked in. She was wearing her uniform, the standard blue-black, complete with gun and club and sagging, over-burdened belt.

"Sorry I'm late," she said.

She blew a big green bubble. Britney noticed that her lips were coated in a shiny layer of clear gloss. Then, spiting her gum into a piece of wrapper she'd kept for this purpose, she said, "So, what's up? What happened, Britney? You sounded hysterical when you called me just now."

"I think I know who it was."

"Oh?" said the detective. "Well, tell me. Please."

"Yeah," Britney said. She fingered the pin on Ricky's letter jacket as she spoke. "I was having sort of a bad night, you know? Just thinking about Ricky a whole lot and feeling really down about everything. Adam was being really annoying, and it seemed like the only way to get any peace was to go off some-where and think for a while."

The detective took notes in a thick leather-bound pad as Britney spoke. "Who's Adam?" she asked.

Britney explained everything. She told the detective who Adam was and how he had caught Bobby spying on her and how she'd gone off to the park to sit and be alone. "You know, that one off Shoreline Drive with all the hiking paths? What's it called? Menominee Park, I think." She told her about how Karl Brown, her friend Melissa's brother, had happened to be there too, looking for the Indian mounds. "I didn't even know there were Indian mounds in that park," she told the detective. She explained how she and Karl had got to talking about random stuff. A friendly conversation—it had cheered her up just to talk about this and that as if everything were normal again. Then out of nowhere, Bobby had come charging up and tried to tackle the guy. "Unless," she concluded, "he was going after me, which is what I think he was doing."

"Well . . ." The detective reviewed her notes. "We can't be sure of anything until we have all the facts. But I'll talk to Bobby. You'll be happy to know I've already spoken with Digger about his conversation with Ricky—I didn't find out much, though. He corroborated what you told me, but he didn't add anything new." She gazed contemplatively at Britney, then reached out to hold her hand.

"You're shaking," she said.

Britney's voice caught in her throat as she tried to say, "Yeah." She slid her hand across the table and let the detective hold it still.

"It must be tough, going through all these emotions again. It must churn up all your feelings about your mother."

Britney couldn't speak. She nodded.

"You know, I worked on her case."

"Really?"

"I didn't do much. I was new to the force at the time. But yeah, I helped out a little bit."

"How come I didn't meet you then?"

"Oh, the stuff I was doing was really low level. I always thought it was sad, though, that they never found her body. Sad for you, I mean. It might have provided you with some closure."

The topic made Britney even more uncomfortable.

"Why didn't you tell me this before?" she asked.

The detective thought for a second. "I figured I should get to know you better first. Like I said, I was really low level. I hardly did anything. Typed up a few reports."

Studying her notes again, the detective tapped her pen on the table.

"Karl Brown. I feel like I've heard that name before."

"He's Melissa's brother," Britney reminder her. "And he was arrested, I don't know, a year and half ago or so in a crystal meth sting."

"That's interesting," the detective said, taking another note. "But I don't work narcotics, so it wouldn't be from that. No, you know what I think it is? I think there was a guy named Karl Brown who worked at the place you guys rented the rafts from."

Britney threw the detective a cockeyed look.

"On that trip . . . with your mother."

"Maybe," Britney said. "It's probably not that uncommon a name."

The thought of Karl being up there the day her mother had died sent a flash of terror and adrenaline suddenly rushing through Britney's bloodstream. What if he had been involved in her mother's death? What if he was coming after her now to finish the . . . No—she couldn't bear to think about that. She reminded herself this didn't have anything to do with her mother.

"Are you going to arrest Bobby?" she asked.

"I don't know as I have enough evidence to do that yet."

"How about this: did you know that he wanted to date me once? I mean, he really laid it on thick. He asked me out probably fifty times and he wouldn't take no for an answer. I finally had to totally cut off all contact with him."

"Before that, you two were friends?"

Britney shrugged. The idea of telling this woman her whole life story disturbed her, especially since she'd worked on her mother's case. It was all just too close.

"That's not the point. The point is, who else could it be? He's *stalking* me. *And* he has a red pickup truck—did you know that? He doesn't drive it all the time because, technically, it belongs to the computer place he works for, but I've seen him riding around in it. Oh, and I found this on the ground while I was talking to him just now!" She handed over the shotgun shell casing she'd picked up. "I think it fell out of his pocket while he was wrestling with Karl."

"So, you think he's the one behind everything."

Britney flinched, hearing those words. "Isn't it obvious?"

"Nothing's obvious, but I'll tell you what: I'm going to check it all out for you."

nineteen

By the time Britney got home, she was a complete wreck. It all seemed so clear. Bobby was stalking her, and Detective Russell should stop him. That's what the police were there for.

Adam didn't look like he'd moved since she left—he was still slouched on the couch, gazing at the TV, which was now showing a rerun of *That 70s Show*.

Throwing Ricky's letter jacket over the arm of the rocking chair—another legacy from her mother's pioneer ancestors—Britney sighed. "Well, that was fun," she said, hoping her sarcasm would captivate Adam's attention.

He ignored her.

"How was the rest of *Alias*?" she asked.

He shrugged. He didn't even look at her.

"Where's my dad?" she asked, noticing the time.

She flopped into the rocking chair and let out another long sigh.

They watched TV together for a while. It was a funny episode, but Britney wasn't in the mood for laughter. She could barely pay attention, actually. Her mind kept wandering back to Bobby Plumley and the pleading, wounded look he'd given her before she turned away from him. It was spooky. She didn't think she was paranoid.

Adam's mood seemed equally sour. On the TV, he watched Red yell and scream and Eric simper without even cracking a smile.

After twenty minutes or so of this, Britney finally tried again. "It's eleven o'clock. Don't you think my dad should be home by now?"

"I don't know? Should he?"

Well, this was a start. Communication, however cursory and combative, was better than silence.

Britney's father sometimes worked on Sundays but never this late. Given the events of the day, she was worried. He was so trusting. This made him such a good defense attorney—his willingness to believe his clients were innocent despite any and all evidence to the contrary—but it also meant that he was capable of stumbling into danger without realizing it until it was too late. She hoped nothing bad had happened to him. When she'd spoken to him after the chaos of the park, he'd said he was at the office. But now that she thought about it, there was maybe too much background noise—shouting voices, muffled music—for him to have been telling the truth.

She called him again now, but she got his voice mail—his phone didn't even ring. He must have turned it off.

"I'm serious, Adam. Do you know where my dad is? He's not answering his phone." She didn't say what she was actually thinking, that maybe whoever was after her—Bobby, obviously Bobby—might have gotten to him on his way home.

"Maybe you should put one of those house arrest doohickeys around his ankle," Adam said.

"You don't have to be like that."

Striding to the window, she searched up and down the street for some sign of him. "Really, don't you think it's weird that he's not home yet?"

The wind whipped snow in long hissing arcs up and over the drifts that had built up along the plowed street. Where could he *be*?

Adam struggled to his feet and joined her at the window. He gazed out with her for a while.

She felt something on her shoulder, not the one near Adam, but the other one, a tapping, like the long finger of death coming for her. She shrieked—"What's that?"— and spun, but no one was there.

Adam chuckled.

She could have killed him.

"Don't *do* that. I thought you were—"

"Who? Bobby Plumley?"

She slapped him. She actually slapped him! She couldn't remember ever slapping a boy before in her life.

He grinned that mischievous grin of his and said, "Okay, you need to relax. And get a sense of humor."

His eyes lingered, waiting for a sign from her. They twinkled, and she felt like she was discovering something about his personality. In a weird way, he was trying to cheer her up.

She didn't know why, but she suddenly felt terribly happy to have Adam around. She burst into laughter, surprising herself as much as she surprised him.

"I didn't know that one worked on anybody anymore," he said. He was laughing as well.

Once they'd calmed down, the two of them returned to their morbid gazing out of the window. Britney contemplated telling Adam about her evening for a moment. Then she thought better of it.

"I think it's weird," she said. "It's making me worried."

"Anyway," Adam said, "it doesn't look like he's coming right now." He wandered back to the couch and poised tensely on the edge, returning his attention to the TV, which was now showing a rerun of *Everybody Loves Raymond*.

Britney came and sat next to him. She was tense too.

They watched the show in absolute silence, and when it was over, they watched the old episode of *Seinfeld* that followed it.

When they heard the car turn into the driveway, they both jumped.

"Oh, thank God," Britney said.

She zapped off the TV.

Her father was drunk. She could tell by the way he tried to

control his posture and carefully place his feet every time he took a step—by how hard he was trying to act like he was sober. Seeing Britney and Adam's expectant gazes, he stopped in the archway that opened into the living room and blinked at them, his eyelids at half-mast. His London Fog trench coat was folded over his arm, his briefcase in his hand. Without really noticing what he was doing, he dropped them where he stood and entered the room. He didn't stumble or lurch—he was a dignified drunk. But Britney knew the signs. In the months immediately following her mother's death, she'd seen him like this more times than she wanted to remember.

"So," he said, "Britney, did you talk to the detective?" His voice took soft curves around the hard consonants.

Adam turned to Britney. "You talked to the detective? About what? About Bobby? I told you, I scared him off." He looked wounded and slightly alarmed.

Choosing to ignore both of their questions, Britney couldn't hide her agitation when she asked her father, "Where have you been? I was scared to death!"

The three off them spoke over and through one another. Mr. Johnson pressed her to find out how her conversation with the detective had gone. Adam complained about her having gone to the detective at all. Their voices were raised. Not so much in anger as in concurrent crosscurrents of anxiety.

To Britney, it felt like the conversation with Detective Russell had taken place ages ago. What was important was finding out what was going on with her father, but the two of them were pressing her too hard for her to get the answers to her own questions.

"Shut up! Okay? Just shut up!" she said finally. "Look, I'm not going to tell you what we talked about, okay? It's private. But Dad, you were right. I feel better now that I saw her. She's a very nice woman. Let's leave it at that. And Adam, if Bobby's in trouble—and I'm not saying he is—it's not your concern. Okay? I'm sure he deserves whatever's coming to him."

"What's that supposed to mean?" Adam asked. "Are you going to get him arrested? Because of what I told you? I don't think you need to do that. He's just a weird, lonely guy."

She spun on him, enraged. "Don't tell me you're going to stick up for him now all of a sudden."

"I'm not sticking up for him. I just think that, you know, people change."

This was all too much. Britney could feel the rage welling inside her. She turned her back on Adam—it was either that or revisit the scene at the Sanctuary. She focused her attention back on her father, who had fallen out and lost track of the conversation. He was sitting in the wing chair, his whole body slack, staring off into the indefinite distance.

"So where were you?" she said again, her voice quivering.

He startled. It took him a moment to fully comprehend her question.

"I was supposed to meet Karl," he said slowly. He sounded exhausted and extremely sad. "We were going to get a quick beer at Capital Brewery. I was going to buy him dinner. I wanted to hear how his new job was going and go over some stuff with him—"

Britney cut him off. "What stuff?"

"Just some stuff about his case. Some stuff I've discovered. I had a few questions for him." Through the drunken glaze in his eyes lurked a profound disappointment—with what, Britney didn't know. "He stood me up, though. We'd said eight-thirty. What time did you call me? A little after nine, right? And he still hadn't arrived. I waited for, I don't know, three or four hours. Until just now. I guess I got a little looped. I . . . He said he had changed. The way he used to be, he was capable of any-thing. He was always on the verge of getting himself in some really ugly situations. I wanted to believe he had changed. I thought he had changed. . . ." Trailing off, Mr. Johnson returned to staring off into space.

"And he never showed up?" Britney asked.

He vaguely shook his head.

"And isn't his case over? I mean, he was sentenced and he went to jail and it's over, right? What new stuff is there to dis-cover?"

Her father's hands described invisible shapes in the air.

"Just . . . things," he said. There was something resigned, broken, in the way he said this.

Britney had no idea what those things were, but she imag-ined that they weren't good. She remembered what the detec-tive had said about a guy with the same name working at that raft rental place when her mother had died, and she shuddered.

twenty

It was four-thirty Monday morning, and Karl was already at work. The sun wouldn't rise for three more hours, and he was alone under the ghostly fluorescents of the Bavarian Brat Haus's packaging center.

He tuned the radio to his favorite station: 102.7, The Viper—classic rock, pure and simple with more music, less talk, and hourly rock blocks to keep you going all day long. Turning the volume up to the max, he spun the nozzle attached to the wall and wheeled out the hose to spray down the room.

He set the hose's spray gun attachment on the nozzle to its most powerful stream. The water spewed out in a strong jet and as it hit, it shoved the dust forward. As the sprayed area grew, a border of black grime developed around its contour. The trick was to spray in an ever-increasing circle, gradually pushing the grime toward the drainage hole in the dead center of the room.

He sang along to the radio as he worked. *La-a-ayla—darling, won't you ease my worried mi-i-i-ind.*

Once the spraying down was done, Karl had to prepare the processing tools. He unhinged the funnel of the first grinder and pulled out the rotating blades, testing their sharpness on his finger as he ran the diamond steel sharpener over them. He did the same with the grinder plates. He repeated this whole process over again with the second grinder. Then the third. Then the fourth.

Sometimes, when the music was especially soulful and deep, he crooned. "Wild Horses." "Open Arms." "Jukebox Hero."

And then it was on to the butchering knives. The boring knives. The breaking knives. The cimeter knives. The skinner knives. The seven-inch carbon steel cleavers.

When he heard the opening few chords of Zep's "Black Dog," he took a break. He pranced around the room, a cleaver in each hand, pretending he was a kung fu master.

Then he laid the knives out in order on the steel tables, one set for each work area.

The Bavarian Brat Haus was a full-service meat-finishing facility. They didn't kill the animals, but they took them from carcass to premium cut and prepared a whole line of specialty sausages: kaiser brats, Numberger brats, kackwurst and knack-wurst and knockwurst and bockwurst and knoblewurst, Wisconsin red brats and classic Sheboygan-style brats, summer sausage, andouille, and, of course, wieners.

For sanitary reasons, they could only make one type of sausage a day, so they packaged on a rotating schedule. Today was the "whites," as Karl had learned to call them. Munich weisswurst, veal and pork mixed with mild, slightly sweet seasonings.

He danced into the walk-in freezer to select the cuts that were needed today.

A gutted cow hung from a hook in the middle of the freezer. Along one wall was a row of halved pigs. Along the opposite wall was a large shelving unit on which were stacked various cuts of veal and beef. The prime meat was too valuable to be used in sausages. What he was looking for were the end parts, the throwaways. These were usually slopped together in large steel vats against the back wall. They weren't there, though, today. That was odd.

As he dragged a canister of bloom gelatin (the binding agent the Brat Haus used for its sausages, which is made up of a mixture of head cheese, souse, and blood tongue) from the freezer, the radio fritzed out.

That was even odder, but he shrugged it off, figuring that there was a short in the cord—it was a cheap old thing, after all.

Once he'd placed gelatin next to each of the grinders, he fidgeted with the radio, trying to get it to work again. The cord was sticky and soft, and by feeling his way down it, he was able to feel the wires running inside the plastic sheathing. Near the plug, there was a short stretch where the wire had been exposed and was taped together with electrician's tape. He stripped this and twisted the wires, trying to get them to form a complete circuit.

"Ow! Shit!"

He gave himself a doozy of a shock.

Giving up on the radio, he returned to the freezer to get the boxes of hog casing that they would need for the sausages.

There was a loud bang, like someone had just smashed a sledgehammer onto the concrete floor, and then the lights went out.

Karl couldn't see anything. He knew his way around pretty well, though, so he carried the first box out into the dark packing room and set it on one of the tables.

The knives he'd laid out were scattered around, no longer in the nice order he'd placed them in. The cleaver was missing. He must have knocked into them in the darkness. But he hadn't heard the cleaver clatter to the floor.

"Hello?" he said, looking around to see if anyone was there.

Silence.

He returned to the freezer for the next box. As he bent to pick it up, something moved behind him.

He spun to see what was there, but he was too late. The cleaver was swinging down toward him—slicing his right arm and knocking him back into the shelving. Frozen veal came falling down onto his head.

Someone stood over him, bundled in a heavy black snowmobile suit, face covered by a hunter orange ski mask.

Struggling to his feet, Karl lunged for his attacker. He wasn't quick enough. The attacker backed away, slashing the air with the cleaver.

Grabbing the first thing he could get his hands on—a frozen veal shank, as it turned out—Karl began swinging wildly. He landed a blow on his attacker's head, which sent both of them tumbling to the concrete floor, but in his weakened state Karl lost his grip on his weapon in the process.

As they rolled around, Karl tried to grab the cleaver from his assailant's hands, but his arm was useless. He was losing a lot of blood. He was getting woozy.

The cleaver flicked through the air. Karl's only defense was to duck and twirl in hopes of staying out of its way, but with each movement, his head grew heavier, his vision became more blurred. He was losing strength quickly.

It finally caught him just above the shoulder blade, severing his carotid artery.

He howled. He clawed at his wounds with his good, left hand. The blood was thick—it froze as soon as it hit the air— but the warm blood pumping out of the open gash in his neck kept coming.

The door slammed shut.

The freezer was pitch black inside.

Karl was cold.

So cold.

Unbearably cold.

twenty-one

Usually Britney had nothing to say to Dr. Yeager, the soft-spoken, middle-aged shrink her father forced her to visit. Her weekly appointment was for Monday morning at nine, which meant she had to miss the first two periods of school. The rules were that she could talk if she wanted to, and if she didn't, she could sit there silently and wait for the hour to tick away.

Her father attended with her—they were in family grief counseling, supposedly to help them deal with her mother's death—and most weeks, he filled up the time with his own stream of consciousness. Memories of playing I Spy on family road trips; of the time Jan ran the Chicago marathon and the hours he put into helping her train, riding his bicycle behind her, spurring her on with encouraging words and carrying her water and PowerBars; of the various times (and he seemed to remember each and every one) when he had let his anxiety over his work create conflict between the two of them.

Sometimes he touched on the psychiatric troubles his wife experienced late in her life, the paranoia and religious fervor, the insomnia and erratic behavior. At these times, his voice fell nearly to a whisper, and the loudest sound in Dr. Yeager's bright office was Britney's anxious sighs of discomfort.

But today, he wasn't there.

She drove to therapy herself, in a separate car from her father, and usually he arrived a good fifteen minutes before she did. The only thing that stopped her from skipping out was that if she did so, he would take the car away from her. It was one of the stipulations he'd laid down when he bought it for her. Seeing that he hadn't bothered to come today, she felt resentful, like she'd somehow been tricked.

To punish him, she'd opened up to Dr. Yeager today. She spent the time complaining about her father. By nine-thirty, when he still wasn't there, she'd begun to repeat herself.

"That's the thing about him," she said. "One little thing, even if it's just a tiny thing, a completely unimportant thing, and it will send him spiraling back into his depression. I mean, so his flaky client stood him up? What does he expect? I mean, Karl? Come on. The guy's a charity case. And he's creepy."

"You've got some strong feelings about Karl," said Dr. Yeager.

Britney shrugged.

Prodding, Dr. Yeager said, "I wonder, do you think maybe

you're jealous of the fact that he's taking up so much of your father's time?"

This was exactly the sort of statement that Britney expected from Dr. Yeager. Hearing him talk this way reminded her why she usually kept her mouth shut in therapy.

She folded her arms across her chest and fumed. But she continued sitting there. She knew that the doctor wouldn't bring anything up, not Ricky, not her mother, nothing, unless she gave him a sense that she'd open up to him. She was going to stay silent until the hour was up, whether to punish the doctor or to punish her father, she wasn't sure.

It was a beautiful day, warm for this time of year—thirty-eight degrees Fahrenheit. Sunlight glimmered off everything—the windshields of the cars in the parking lot, the snowbanks piled up on the side of the road. The telephone wires looping along overhead were crusted in a thin layer of ice; they shimmered like bands of silver.

The minutes seemed to drag on.

Britney stared at the walls, which were painted a fluffy blue and decorated with intentionally soothing posters of impressionist paintings: Seurat's *Sunday in the Park,* Monet's *Water Lilies.* The bookshelf contained a whole collection of self-help books—she'd stared at these titles many times before.

Dr. Yeager broke the silence. "Have you thought about your mom at all recently? I'd think, given all that's happened, some of those old wounds might have opened up."

If she were going to be honest, she would have to admit that it was true, she *had* thought about her mom. The rampant fear she'd been experiencing since Ricky's death was made worse by her worries that she might just be paranoid, more like her mother than she wanted to believe. But she couldn't allow Dr. Yeager the satisfaction of hearing her admit he was right.

"No," she mumbled, clicking her jaw.

The silence was excruciating. She wondered, where was her father? This tardiness was becoming a habit.

Finally the chime of her cell phone bailed her out. It was him.

"Where are you?" she said.

"I'm not going to make it." His voice was muffled. Britney could barely make out what he was saying.

"Why not?"

The long silence on the other end of the line made Britney think she'd lost him for a moment, but he finally said, "I'm over here at Mr. and Mrs. Brown's house. Melissa's here too. I can't really talk right now, so I'm going to come right out and say it. There's been an . . . accident."

Before he even told her what it was, Britney felt the muscles around her stomach clench, as though it were preparing for a punch in the gut.

She lowered her voice. "Oh my God, what?"

Dr. Yeager was watching her as she spoke. She tipped her head and tried to cradle the phone away from his gaze.

"Karl. He . . . he was found murdered this morning over at the Brat Haus."

Britney grimaced. She didn't want to give a single emotion away to the doctor.

"Uh-huh," she said.

"So I'm going to be over here most of the morning helping. I'm sorry, Pumpkin. I got the call as I was driving over and I haven't had a chance to get to you until just now."

"It's okay," she lied. She was shaking.

"Do you want to talk to Melissa for a second? I know she'd appreciate hearing your voice."

"Uh, okay." She told herself, Hold it together, hold it together.

Melissa's tears almost made Britney feel like she was going begin sobbing as well.

"You're one of the strongest people I know," Britney said, trying to find the words that might best console Melissa. "You'll get through this. I promise. If you need me for any-thing—anything at all—I'll be here. Okay?"

Melissa murmured, "Thanks," and quickly said she had to go. She was too upset to talk.

"Don't forget, okay? You've been there for me every time, and if . . ." Knowing there were no words to take Melissa's pain away, she said, "I love you, Melissa. I'll see you soon."

When she hung up, Britney didn't know where to look. She knew that Dr. Yeager was staring at her. She didn't want to return his gaze. She settled on the mobile hanging in the corner above the window—dark-stained wooden blocks cut into odd geometric shapes.

"Is everything okay?" asked the doctor.

Britney couldn't stop herself. "No, everything's not okay!" she shouted, finally releasing all the panic and fear that had been building up inside her. "Someone's out to get me! Do you understand that? What happened to Ricky . . . And Karl's dead now . . . It's all part of their larger plan!"

He jotted something down in the folder on his desk.

"How does that make you feel?" he said calmly.

"You know, what? Forget it." She covered her face with her hands and moaned. "You people all just think I'm crazy like my mom!"

twenty-two

Melissa's parents had offered to come along to help clean out Karl's meager belongings, but Melissa had insisted on doing it alone. Now here she was in her dead brother's apartment. Her relationship with Karl had always been troubled. She thought packing up his stuff, holding each item in her hands, looking at the refuse left of his life one parcel at a time, would help her understand him better.

Mr. Johnson, who was taking care of everything for Melissa's family, even going so far as to work out the funeral arrangements, had dropped her off in the parking lot behind the complex where Karl had lived. Just seeing the place had made Melissa's heart throb. It was so chintzy. A two-story yellow-brick development behind the multiplex off the Washington Avenue strip—nondescript in every way. She couldn't imagine how anyone could live here without being terribly lonely.

"Are you sure you don't want any help?" Mr. Johnson had said.

"No. It's okay. I sort of want to do this by myself," she said.

He had handed her a set of keys.

"You see that truck over there?" he'd said, pointing at a beat-up red Ford sitting all alone in the far corner of the parking lot. "That's Karl's. You'll probably be able to fit all his things in the back."

Not even knowing what his car looked like made her feel terrible. It was sad. She'd paid so little attention to Karl since his getting out of jail. This was the first time she'd even been to his apartment.

The front room was moderately small. It was nearly completely empty and carpeted in an ugly beige. There were no curtains on the windows, no art on the walls, no bookshelves or stereo or television.

What it contained was this: a fold-up card table; a beach chair; a stack of well-thumbed books by Elmore Leonard and Jim Thompson; a CD/cassette boom box with a broken antenna, missing the door to the cassette player; and a few other sundry things. Nothing of any real value. Paper plates and plastic silverware. Half a mushroom pizza, still in its box on the counter.

She recognized his imprint on the space. The empty tallboys of Miller Genuine Draft stacked in a pyramid in the windowsill. Lying on the floor, the baseball signed by Paul Molitor and Robin Yount that he'd cherished since he was a child.

It was hard to imagine what he did with his time here. The image of him slouched back in the beach chair, dirty jeans hanging low on his hips, his naked shoulders and back scratching against the white and green strips of vinyl, a beer in one hand and a cigarette in the other, staring at the wall, staring and staring and waiting for his brain to tell him it was tired—this was what she imagined the substance of his life had been like since he'd been released.

The room stank of sadness, and to think that this sadness was related to her, it was too much to bear.

There were tears in her eyes now.

She was startled to find a shotgun leaning against the wall behind the bedroom door. She wondered where he got it and what kind of trouble he could have been in. Maybe he hadn't reformed himself as much as Mr. Johnson claimed he had. For some reason, the gun didn't scare her so much as make her feel even sadder for her brother.

Other than the gun, the bedroom was nearly empty. A mess of clothes in the corner. A futon, a shoe box stuffed with documents. Rummaging through the box, Melissa found Karl's birth certificate, his social security card, his release papers.

There were letters in the box as well.

The one on top, decorated with florid drawings of pursed lips and cupid hearts, read:

Dear Karl,

It's Valentine's Day and you're in there and I'm out here. It's not fair. I wish I could at least come to visit you. I can't, obviously. It would be too risky. But all day today I've been imagining what I'd do if I could. Remember that day when we drove out into the country and found that abandoned farmhouse? Do you remember what we did when we got there? I wish I could do that with you today.

That's not all I would do, though. If I could, I'd put on that Victoria's Secret slip you bought me—the black lacy one that barely comes down to my thighs. And I'd wear the silky red thong you like so much, or maybe I wouldn't. I guess it would depend on how good a boy you were. I'd sashay my hips and dance in front of you, teasing you until you couldn't stand it. You wouldn't be allowed to touch me. That would be the rule. Not until I said it was okay . . .

The letter went on to describe an extremely sensual situation. It was so graphic that Melissa flushed. She felt like she was doing something unethical by intruding like this. She knew she should stop reading, put the letter back in the box, and pack the whole thing up with Karl's other things, let his prison letters remain secret and his, but she couldn't.

The script the letter was written in was vaguely familiar. She'd seen it before, but she couldn't place it.

It was unsigned.

There were many more letters like this in the box. All of them sexy. None of them signed.

She racked her brain, trying to place where she'd seen this handwriting before, but she couldn't remember.

As she continued digging to the bottom of the box, she dreaded what she might find there.

In a sudden rush of memory, she knew where she'd seen the handwriting on the letters before. At Britney's house. Hundreds of times, on little notes left on the kitchen table reminding the girls that there were cookies in the rabbit jar or lemonade in the fridge, on permission slips for school trips, on all the various scraps of paper that parents leave trailing behind their children.

It was Jan Johnson's handwriting. Britney's mother. But she'd died before Karl was sent to prison.

Then she felt something small clinging to the bottom of the shoe box.

A Polaroid.

She was afraid to look at it.

twenty-three

Adam noticed as soon as he saw Melissa that she looked hollowed out, her eyes sunken and dark, like they'd seen things that had turned them prematurely old, her posture broken as though she had been dragging a boulder behind her all day. Her curly red hair was more unruly than usual, sticking up everywhere.

Her parents were sitting together at the cluttered table in the living room. They each had a stack of books in front of them, but neither was reading. It was hard to tell what they were doing, actually. They looked shell-shocked, harrowed. As though they'd been staring off into space for an eternity of hours and Adam's ringing of the doorbell had blasted them back from their dark reverie; they seemed confused about where they were.

Melissa barely stopped to acknowledge them. She nodded his way and said, "This is Adam, Britney's friend." Then she ushered him upstairs so quickly that he had time to do nothing but grimace and wave.

Locking the door behind them, she kicked a path through the clothes piled in the middle of the floor and shoved the open notebooks and loose-leaf papers to the side of the bed, making room for the two of them to sit side by side.

Then she started sobbing.

Cupping her hands loosely, tenderly between his palms, Adam said nothing. He watched her, waiting.

Death seemed unreal to him. He'd never known anybody who'd died—well, he'd known Britney's mom, but he hadn't been here for that. He'd heard about it from his parents one day when he got home from school. It had made him sad, but he hadn't seen Jan Johnson for years and it had just been news from the world outside his reality at the time. When he'd arrived here in Madison, her absence had seemed strange for a few weeks, but it hadn't been shocking. It hadn't turned his world upside down.

When Ricky died, Adam had felt bad for Britney, even though he didn't know how to show it, and remembering the way his jokey behavior had upset her, he tried now with Melissa to be more appropriately somber.

Before leaving work at Amoeba, he'd bought her a CD with his employee discount, *It's a Wonderful Life* by Sparklehorse. It had come out a while ago, but it was still one of his favorites—

not many people had heard of the band, and they were haunting and mournful and very, very cool. The perfect thing to remind her that she wasn't alone in her sadness.

"Do you have a CD player?" he asked.

She nodded and pointed to the Discman balanced precariously on the windowsill.

They listened reverently to the dirge-like songs on it.

After a couple of songs, she said, "It's good." A brief smile broke across her face, but it quickly dissolved.

When she'd called him at work to tell him about her brother, she'd said she had something else important she needed to talk to him about. Her voice had been clipped, strained with the effort to hold her emotions in.

"What is it?" he'd asked.

"I can't tell you now."

"Why not?"

"It's . . . you know . . . my parents are here." There was a shuffling noise on the other end of the line, and then Melissa whispered into the phone, "I found something. While I was cleaning out Karl's apartment. It's . . . I'm really freaked out."

The dread and not knowing had rattled him for the rest of the evening. He couldn't imagine what she might have found. A journal full of murderous confessions? A message written in blood on the wall? Child pornography? Every idea that slid through his mind seemed far-fetched. And none of them explained why she had to keep everything secret.

The whole walk over, he'd prepared himself to listen, told

himself not to judge the things she might say to him, to be prepared for anything. That's what he'd thought Melissa wanted from him.

Now, beneath the dim shaded lamp on the bedside table of her messy bedroom, he asked her, "How are you feeling? Is there anything . . . What can I do?"

The tears came pouring out of her, as though she'd been saving them all up for this moment.

She buried her head in his shoulder, and he held her, rubbing her back lightly with his fingertips.

After she'd calmed down, she looked up at him. Her face was pink. Her freckles were darker, angry splotches of red screaming from her nose.

With the back of his finger, he wiped the tears from her cheeks. They were surprisingly cold. He wanted to give her a tissue to wipe her nose with, but he couldn't find one in her cluttered room.

After a while, when she could finally get out some halting words, she said, "I'm so scared. Who would want to do this? Karl was a messed-up guy, but he wasn't a *bad* guy. He was just . . . Whoever is doing this, it seems like it doesn't matter who you are; they don't care."

Her shoulders shook as she sobbed, and Adam tried his best to hold her steady.

She looked him dead in the eye.

"Do you know anything about guns?" she said.

Hearing this question, he startled and recoiled slightly from her. He wondered what she knew about his last few months in New Hampshire and how she could have learned it. "A little," he said. "Why? Does this have to do with the thing you couldn't tell me?"

Nodding, she slid from the bed and dug into the darkness of her closet, pulling out a shotgun.

Adam's eyebrows rose. He was disturbed, but he was also relieved; this had nothing to do with him. "Where'd you get that?"

"It was in Karl's apartment."

From the way she waved the gun around, she obviously didn't have any experience with firearms.

"Whoa! Whoa!" Adam said, as calmly as he could. "Watch where you point that thing! Here, let me see it."

Examining the gun, he recognized the make and model. It was a Winchester Super X2 Greenhead.

"Do you know where he got it?"

Melissa shook her head.

He pointed out a small dot of Wite-Out on the hilt. "You see that? That's the way Mr. Johnson marks his hunting rifles."

"How do you know that?"

"He showed them to me a month or so ago. He's got two of them." A flash of disturbance flew briefly across her face, and hoping to reassure her that he and Mr. Johnson had a legitimate reason to be playing with the guns, he said, "Back in New Hampshire, I was a big hunter. See, look at my coat. It's a duck-hunting jacket."

She nodded gravely. She was nervously tapping her knuckles against her lips.

"Does he know you found this?" asked Adam.

"No." She started rummaging around in the closet again, looking for something. "There's this other thing too," she said. "Let me just find it."

"Does Detective Russell know?"

"No."

"Well, you should definitely tell her. But I don't know, maybe you should hold off on telling Mr. Johnson."

"Why?"

She looked suspicious suddenly, and he scrambled to explain. "I mean, can you imagine how much more upset Britney would be if she found out about this? She's already a nervous wreck."

Melissa stopped her search through the closet suddenly. For a second, she played with the rim of her glasses, like she was calculating something in her head. Then her face broke and scrunched in on itself and she started sobbing again.

Adam reached out to touch her shoulder, and she wrapped her arms around him, clutching him tightly. Her head was buried in his collarbone. He could feel her tears soaking through his T-shirt.

"It's okay," he said. "It's okay, it's okay, it's okay. I've got you."

Then he felt something else, something unmistakable. She'd kissed his neck.

He squeezed her more tightly, ran his fingers through her hair, and somehow, he was suddenly kissing her back and she had her hands under his T-shirt and he had his hands under her sweatshirt and they weren't sitting up anymore—they were lying down, and Melissa's skin was so soft and her hands so tender and when she said his name—"Adam"—he realized she wasn't crying anymore.

twenty-four

The party that weekend was crazy insane. Saturday night at Troy's place and the music was shaking the walls. His mother's *Wind in the Willows* collector plates rattled on their nails—two had already fallen loose, and there were shards of ceramic everywhere, which nobody bothered to clean up. Troy didn't care, so why should anyone else?

The Raccoons had won again, trouncing their crosstown rivals, the Eisenhower Generals.

Britney had been distracted throughout the game. All she could think about was the murders. She felt, everywhere she went, that people were staring at her and whispering about her, that she was being evaluated for weakness and someone, she didn't know who—Bobby? Someone else?—was waiting for her to let down her guard, at which point they'd attack.

In preparation for the celebration, Erin had spent all afternoon making Jell-O shots in the school colors, red and gold. She'd made six pans' worth, almost a hundred shots, but they were a huge hit and even this copious amount had only lasted half an hour. The red ones turned your tongue crimson and the yellow ones turned your tongue brown.

"Come on, Britney," Erin said. "If there's anyone who needs a drink right now, it's you."

Britney wasn't so sure. "Do you have any idea how upset I am?" she asked.

"We're all upset. That's why we're escaping into alcohol." Erin winked at Britney.

Against her better judgment, Britney consented to a Jell-O shot. "I want a red one," she said. It was the first time she'd had alcohol since her mother died, but given what she'd been through over the past couple of weeks, she felt, maybe Erin was right, maybe she deserved to let go a little bit.

She didn't feel the effects right away, but later, when she found herself on Jeremy's shoulders, her legs braced under his massive biceps, trying to topple Daphney off Digger's shoulders, it hit her that she was in an altered state. She felt bold. She felt free. She was laughing and shrieking and the voice in her head telling her to dread everything and everyone, to be vigilant because danger was always around the next corner, had stopped.

She grappled with Daphney, the two of them pushing and pulling and straining for leverage and trying to avoid knocking their heads on the overhead light. Daphney had played this game many times before. Britney saw that she knew all the moves: how to twist her arm so it remained lower than Britney's, where to turn and when to dodge so that Britney lost her equilibrium. But for Britney, it was another first—one of the many things she would never have been willing to do if she had remained sober.

She didn't last long up in the air, but when she fell, she jumped right up and was ready to go again.

It was fun. Everybody formed a circle around the fighters and cheered.

By her third match, Britney finally got the hang of it. She toppled Cindy, but then she lost to Jodi and the crowd started to find other things to do, so they all retired and sat gossiping on the couch.

"Hey, doesn't that guy who died this week's sister go to La Follette?" asked Daphney.

"I think she does," Jodi said.

"Melissa," Britney said. "She's a friend of mine." Then, embarrassed, she modified this. "I mean, we hung out some-times. Things like that. I still drive her to school every once in a while. She's okay."

"So, did you know this guy who died?"

"Uh-huh."

"God," said Cindy. "It's spooky. First Ricky, now your friend's brother. How can you handle it?"

The girls were all waiting for her answer. "I don't know," she said. "I really don't know."

"Well, I know one way," said Erin, coming to her rescue. "Drown your sorrows!" She held up her can of Bud Light and rattled it teasingly.

Britney felt a little woozy. When the other girls headed toward the kitchen to see what their boyfriends were up to, she told them to go without her. "I just want to sit here for a while," she said.

She scanned the party, sizing up all the usual suspects: the Hummus guys, the preppies, Art Richter, that drug dealer, wondering, Is it him? Or is it him? What about him? Is one of the people in this room with me the one I need to watch out for? None of them appeared to be paying any special attention to her, but how could she be sure?

The music seemed too loud, and it sounded distorted. When the school president, Travis Lawson, leaned in to pat her on the shoulder and say, "How you holding up?" he came in and out of focus, making her head spin. She wished that she hadn't had that Jell-O shot.

She heard a lot of shouting coming from the kitchen. She concentrated, trying to pick the sound apart and figure out what was going on. It was chaotic: dull thuds and cackles, and she thought she heard Cindy shrieking.

Running in to see what was going on, she found the hockey players and their wives in a circle around the island counter, hunched over and chanting, "Do it. Do it. Do it."

Britney screamed, "What happened? Did you get him?"

There was sudden silence. They all turned toward her like she was crazy.

Then Troy started laughing. They all started laughing.

"Relax, Britney," said Erin. "We're doing body shots."

Jeremy leered at her. "You want to do one?" he asked.

Now she could see what was going on. Cindy was laid on the kitchen counter, her halter top pulled up to expose her stomach. Digger had a shot glass full of dark liqueur in his hand and he was precariously trying to balance it on Cindy's belly button. Britney watched as Erin, her hands clasped behind her back, bent over Cindy and clenched the shot glass between her lips, flinging her head back and downing the liquid in one quick swallow.

"See?" she said as she pounded the empty glass down on the counter. "It's fun. You should try it."

"What? Did you think someone was trying to kill me?" asked Cindy, and everyone laughed again.

Britney felt so dizzy.

"I don't feel so good," she said.

Then she collapsed onto the floor.

twenty-five

At about the same time that Britney was swallowing her Jell-O shot, Melissa sat at Fresh Grounds with Bobby Plumley, killing time until Adam got off work. She hovered over her hot chocolate like it was a campfire. He was drinking a triple-shot latte, which she thought was a crazy thing to do at nine-thirty at night—then again, this was Bobby Plumley; she'd seen him do a lot weirder things than this.

She was telling him about the discovery she'd made at Karl's apartment. She hadn't discussed it with anyone all week. The truth was that she trusted Bobby, and with his hacker skills and his sharp mind, she figured he could help her figure the whole thing out.

"The letters aren't even the most disturbing thing," she whispered, leaning across the table so no one could hear but him.

"Well, tell me, then," he said. "Or do you want me to guess?"

He was in one of his moods, snapping at everything she said and generally being unpleasant. He'd chosen a particularly obnoxious T-shirt to wear today: I'm Running Out of Places to Hide the Bodies, it read.

Throughout the week, Melissa had been shaking uncontrollably at random times—while taking her vocab quiz in Ms. Straub's class, while waiting in line for the chin-up bar in gym. It was as if whenever she thought she had finally put Karl out of her mind and escaped thinking about those spooky letters from Britney's mother, her body rebelled against her and forced her morbid fears back into her brain.

"Okay, so inside the shoe box, under the letters, there was . . . this thing." She cast Bobby a long, meaningful look.

"Jesus, Melissa, either tell me or don't tell me, but stop toying with me, all right?"

"A photograph," she said. "There was a photo of Britney."

"So?"

"She was naked in it."

Bobby smirked and stared at her, like he was still waiting for her to get to the point.

"I'm serious, Bobby, it's really disturbing."

"Why are you telling me all this?" he asked. He seemed pissed. He got this way whenever Britney's name came up in conjunction with another guy.

"Oh, grow up, Bobby. This is important. Don't you think it's weird?" Melissa reminded herself to stay calm, to regulate her voice so that she didn't draw attention to their conversation. "Britney's mother's writing letters to my brother—after she's supposedly already dead—and Britney is sending him nude photos of herself."

"Yeah, I guess it's a little weird."

"So, what do you think it means?"

"How should I know?"

She shot him a knowing look. He knew as well as she did how stormy Britney's relationship with her mom had been.

"I mean," he said, "it's obvious. Either her mom's still alive somehow, or Britney was having an affair with your brother." He squirmed uncomfortably.

"Or both," said Melissa with a grimace.

"Have you told her father?"

"Adam told me I shouldn't. There's another thing. I found a gun in Karl's room too, and Adam says he thinks it belonged to Mr. Johnson."

His right eyebrow rose until she couldn't see it anymore behind his shaggy hair. "You told Adam about all this? Why? When? You've been hanging out with him?"

Crossing her arms, she stared Bobby down.

He tipped his head like he was putting all the pieces together. His eyes slowly narrowed into tiny slits. "Don't tell me—"

"Yeah." She couldn't help smiling. Since that first kiss on Monday night, she'd seen Adam every single day. Not just at school. Everywhere. Every chance they got, they found each other. It was amazing. The only bright spot in her life at the moment.

"Figures," said Bobby.

He stared into his coffee cup for a while and then downed his drink in a single shot. Before he became obsessed with Britney, Bobby had had a crush on Melissa. They'd even kissed one summer night a year and a half ago out at the Sanctuary, but though she liked and respected him, she hadn't been able to muster the interest necessary to date him. There just weren't any sparks. They'd managed to move on from that awkward kiss and stay friends, but she knew Bobby still thought about it sometimes.

After a while he asked, "Can I see the gun?"

"I gave it to Detective Russell."

"Why'd you do that?"

"Why wouldn't I do that?"

Bobby sulked for a while, and then he said, "If I were you, I wouldn't trust Adam as far as I could throw him."

"You sound jealous, Bobby."

Bobby shrugged. "What does Britney say about him?"

"Nothing. She told me he got in a whole bunch of trouble when he was living in New Hampshire, but she didn't say she hated him or anything."

"What kind of trouble?" Bobby asked. He was suddenly interested in the conversation, hunched forward and eager to hear what Melissa had to say.

"I don't know."

"You don't know?"

"I just said, I don't know."

"You hooked up with the guy; don't you think you should learn a little about him?"

Sometimes being with Bobby was so exasperating.

"You know, Bobby, if you dislike him so much, why are you here? Why are you waiting around for him with me?"

"Because I don't have anything better to do. And now that I know he got in 'trouble'"—he put quotation marks around the word with his fingers—"in New Hampshire, I want to keep my eye on him."

"Well, don't do me any favors."

"I'm not planning on doing you any favors," he said.

"What's that supposed to mean?" She could feel her blood rising in her chest. Fighting with Bobby Plumley. She felt bad enough about her brother's death, and now she had to put up with this. What a way to spend a Saturday night!

Bobby motioned with his head toward the door.

"Speak of the devil," he said. And then almost as an afterthought, "Hey, I was just messing with you, okay?"

"Sure, Bobby, whatever."

The plan was to go to a concert at the Tick Tick Boom club. Some local band that none of them had ever heard of before. Black Breasted Robin. Amoeba had been helping sell tickets for the event, and Adam had heard from the guys at the record store that the band was good. He'd procured three free tickets that afternoon—one of the perks of the job—and they'd all been looking forward to checking out the show.

Now, though, Melissa was dreading it. The only reason she didn't back out was that she was afraid of the dark places her head might go if she sat home alone with herself too long.

The three of them piled into Bobby's red pickup.

It was going to be a long, long night.

twenty-six

Madison Arena was an odd place to meet, but since Melissa wanted to know what her friend had to tell her, she hadn't thought twice about making the trek over at twelve-thirty the next night.

Now she was there, in the middle of the rink, slipping back and forth across the red line and waiting. It was freezing. She could feel the chill from the ice right through her snow boots.

Her friend hadn't shown up yet. This seemed odd too.

She figured the news must have something to do with her brother. What other reason would there be for all this secrecy? Whatever it was, it better be good because the hockey arena was spooky all empty and dark like this. It was full of shadows, and when she'd shouted, "Hello? I'm here!" as she'd walked in, her voice had echoed for a long time against the concrete walls.

The scoreboard that had been shot up still hung there in tatters. It looked like a gutted animal. A wide circle of ragged holes marked its face where the shot had lacerated the sheet metal facing. Red and green wiring dangled from it. Attached to one of these wires was a rectangular box full of lightbulbs; it read Visitors across the top.

She wondered if she should whip out her cell and try to track down her friend. The longer she waited here, the more spooked she got. Fumbling in her purse, she finally found the phone. She flipped through the names until she found the one she wanted.

Just as she was about to push send, a door crashed shut. The sound reverberated around the large empty space.

She dropped her phone.

Reaching down to pick it up, she was startled again when the floodlights all came on at once.

She called out, "Hello?"

She was blinded by the bright white glare from the ice and, when she looked up, from the lights overhead.

There was a low humming, like the sound of a car idling, coming from the goal end of the arena.

By the time Melissa's eyes adjusted, she saw that the Zamboni had been driven onto the ice. There was movement behind it, and she called out again, "Is that you?"

Someone ran around the edge of the Zamboni and jumped into the cab, so fast that Melissa couldn't catch who it was—all she saw was a flash of black snowmobile suit.

Standing at center ice, she cursed herself for having come here tonight.

The Zamboni slowly began to roll forward.

She stood stock-still, watching, waiting, hoping beyond hope that this was some sort of exhibition, a dramatic entrance meant to impress her.

And then the Zamboni began picking up speed. It was headed straight for her.

She ran.

But it was hard to run. Her boots had no traction, and the ice was slick.

She made it to the edge of the rink, but where was she supposed to go from there? It was surrounded by a twelve-foot-high ring of glass. Think fast, think fast, she told herself as she jumped out of the way of the huge machine plowing toward her. She barely dodged it. It crashed into the wall, leaving a dent but not shattering the glass, not breaking through the thick wood railing.

And then she was off again, sticking close to the wall, trailing her hand along it in search of an opening. Nothing, nothing, nothing, nothing—even the penalty boxes were closed off to her. They'd been locked from the inside. There was no escape.

Thinking that the Zamboni must have left an opening where it came in, she raced toward the place where she'd first seen it. She slipped and fell face-first, slid a good twelve feet, arms stretched out in front of her.

It was gaining ground.

She tried to scramble up onto her feet, but she kept slipping again, kept falling. She was flailing around.

Then the Zamboni was right there behind her.

She pulled herself forward, tried to crawl away, but it was faster than her. It was right on top of her. She rolled to the right to evade its massive wheels.

As it caught her left foot, she screamed out in pain. The crunching of bones and muscle made a grisly sound, but she didn't have time to check out her wounds. She'd barely escaped, and the Zamboni was turning around now.

On her feet again, she limped toward the goal end of the rink. It seemed so far away. Miles and miles away. She was breathing heavily. Her foot throbbed, and she had a cramp in her side.

She was moving so slowly, then she was on her face again, pushed there by a nudge of the Zamboni against the back of her thighs.

This time she didn't have the energy to spin out from under it. Her right foot was the first thing to get caught in the rotor blades under the tractor's back end. They sliced her rubber boot to shreds and tore through her flesh.

So tired, exhausted now, she knew she couldn't escape. But she didn't give up. She kept struggling, clawing at the ice and pulling against the twirling blades sucking her in.

"Why?" she screamed "Why are you doing this? I never did anything to hurt you!" Her voice was swallowed up in the revving of the blades.

From the cab of the Zamboni came this response: "You really don't know why I'm doing this, Melissa? But I thought you knew everything. Use that big brain of yours. I'm sure you'll figure it out."

twenty-seven

The snow had begun to melt in the few days of unseasonably warm weather that blew through during the second week of February. Islands of slush had formed in the layers of ice, dry-bed rivers, like ant trails, wending between them. The snowbanks had begun to shrink, hardening into small craggy mounds, encrusted with black honeycombs of dirt.

Stubbing her cigarette out in the waterlogged steel trough by the door, Tara Russell stepped inside Madison Arena to check out the damage. She liked to evaluate her crime scenes in solitude. It helped her think.

Lately, she'd been thinking a lot and coming up with nothing.

As she made her way through the fluorescent-lit cinder block tunnel that led to the cavernous rink inside the arena, she mulled over the facts again. Ricky Piekowski. Karl Brown. Their deaths seemed unconnected, yet at the same time, how could they be? No matter how hard she tried, she couldn't figure out what the connection was. Both of them were close to the Johnson family but in completely different contexts, in completely different ways.

That kid Bobby Plumley was interesting to her. He owned a red Ford Ranger, which, from the forensic evidence, was the kind of truck that had killed Ricky. And he obviously had an unnatural fixation on Britney. After what she'd heard from Britney, she'd spoken to him and since then, she'd been keeping a loose eye on him. She had enough evidence to get a judge to slap a restraining order on him, keeping him away from Britney, but she didn't want to do that just yet. At this point, she figured he was just your garden-variety creep.

Anyway, he had an alibi for the night Ricky Piekowski had died: he'd been with Melissa Brown, playing Vice City in her living room. Melissa had corroborated this, and her parents had also said Bobby had been there, at least until they'd gone to bed at ten-thirty.

Another person she was suspicious of was Adam Saft. She found it interesting that all this mischief had begun so soon after his arrival in town, that he'd been so conveniently nearby when Britney had found that CD in her car. The gun that Melissa had found in Karl's apartment had turned out to be registered to Ed Johnson, and Tara found how much Adam knew about Mr. Johnson's guns unnerving. It was conceivable, though as yet unprovable, that Adam and Karl had been up to something.

Of course, this same evidence could just as easily point toward Ed Johnson himself. And the connection between Mr. Johnson and Karl Brown was extensive and well documented. The shotgun shell that Britney had given her had matched the ones used to shoot up the scoreboard above her head—and both of them were a match for the gun belonging to Mr. Johnson that Melissa had discovered in Karl's apartment. Tara had begun to wonder if there were some dark agreement between Ed Johnson and Karl, trailing all the way back to the death of Mr. Johnson's wife—the fact that Karl had worked at that raft rental company was a little too coincidental for her comfort. But why? She saw no motive for Mr. Johnson.

The whole thing gave her a headache.

Inside the arena, Tara was confronted with a grisly trail of destruction.

A wide, solid path of blood trailed down the center of the ice like a red carpet laid out for an awards ceremony. It was not only frozen, it was embedded, saturating the ice the way the regulation paint did.

A trail of shredded clothing was strewn along the edges of the path—a ski jacket, its white synthetic stuffing strewn everywhere, bits of brown corduroy, the strips of pink nylon that looked like they had once been the straps of a bra, chunks of cotton and wool. All of it was soaked through with blood. Some of it had clumps of curly red hair clinging to it.

At the end of this path sat the Zamboni, a small tractor dragging a squeegee behind it. Attached to the front of the tractor was a large water tank. The water inside was red—somehow the victim's blood had been pumped into it.

She had to kneel down to see it, but there was a body after all. Or most of a body. A mess of dismembered parts, internal organs spilling every which way, more clothing in larger pieces—a thick dark shellac of blood poured over all of it. The body was jammed into the metal shield at the rear of the Zamboni, caught like chicken bones in the corkscrew blade that was contained there.

Though it was disfigured and mutilated, the head was still in one piece. She'd have to get someone in to identify it, but Tara already recognized the features.

Melissa Brown.

After touring the rest of the facility, Tara could pretty much tell what had happened.

Somehow the killer had gotten the Zamboni out of its locked shed and driven it out onto the ice. He'd also somehow lured Melissa here. Once he had her on the ice, he had locked off all the exits. Then it was a simple matter of chasing her around the arena until she got tired, tripping her up, and running her over. Once she'd been yanked into the ice-shaving blade at the rear of the machine, there hadn't been any hope left for her. The more she struggled, the farther she must have been pulled in. She'd been ripped to shreds. But that hadn't been enough. The killer had kept going, grinding her into a bloody pulp that had contaminated the water tank and then been spewed out the rear of the Zamboni in a sheet of liquid that was then smoothed down into a new layer of ice by the squeegee.

Another innocent lost, Detective Tara Russell thought. And I'm no nearer to solving this case than I was before the poor girl died.

twenty-eight

For many long hours, Britney watched the light from the window creep across her bedroom wall.

Time passed so slowly. She felt like she was floating underwater, like her bed was keeling in strong ocean currents, being carried deeper and deeper into a dark, rocky cavern where she was all alone. She felt like she'd be stuck there, unable to move, waiting, waiting for her torturer to find her. There was no escape. All she could do now was try not to suffocate in dread.

A soft rapping on her bedroom door woke Britney from this reverie.

"Come—" She cleared her throat. "Come in."

She could tell it was Adam by the shape of his silhouette in the dim hall light.

For some reason she couldn't quite explain to herself, she was happy to see him.

"Is it okay if I sit with you for a while?" he asked. His voice was hoarse, barely a whisper.

"Sure."

He sat on the lip of her bed, his hands in his lap, and stared off into the darkness. In the moonlight, Britney could see the side of his face. His eyes were puffy. He'd been crying, though he wasn't crying now.

She watched him for a while. He didn't move and he didn't speak. She wished he'd do something obnoxious, pull one of his mock-cute moves—it would make things feel a little more normal. He just sat there, though, in a daze.

"I can't believe she's gone," she said finally, the thought carrying in from a long ways away.

"Yeah, me neither."

"I feel like it's my fault."

The look in his eyes as he latched onto hers was more earnest than she'd ever seen from him. "It's not your fault."

"It is," she said. "All of this is my fault. It's like just by existing, I make horrible things happen to everybody around me."

He shook his head.

"It's always been that way. If my mother was here, you could ask her. She knew."

Britney hesitated, wondering how much she should tell Adam about her mother.

"She used to tell me all the time. She called me Chaos. She'd tap me on the chest and say, 'You can't hide the trouble in there from me.'"

"That doesn't sound so bad."

How could she explain the torture she went through with her mother, the mixture of hatred and fear that sometimes stole across her mother's face when she looked at her?

"It was bad. It was horrible. She told me that there was something wrong with me—that I was sick. Not physically sick. Sick in another way. All rotted inside. When I was a little girl, she'd start crying sometimes and I'd get scared and ask why and she'd say she was thinking about all the ways I was going to hurt her one day."

Adam took her hand. "Britney," he said, "you're not sick. Okay? She's the one who was sick."

"Look what's happening! Everyone I know is dying! If it wasn't for me, they'd all still be alive!" The tears were running down her face now. "You know? Everything would be fine if I just wasn't here!"

Taking her other hand, Adam squeezed hard on both of them, like he thought by tightening his grasp, he could forcibly pull her back from the brink.

"You didn't kill anybody, Britney," he said firmly. "It's scary as hell, I know, but you can't blame yourself. That's just what whoever is doing this wants!"

"But it's true," she said, her face contorting with the effort to control her tears. "It's like with my mother. The whole point of going was to try and do something fun as a family, to distract us from all my mom's problems. And right up to the time we left, she kept trying to cancel it. You know why? Because she knew. She told me. We had a big fight right before we left and she said, 'This is it, Britney. One of us . . .'" She couldn't go any further; the tears overwhelmed her.

Adam had her by the shoulders. He squeezed her tight until her shaking subsided.

"`One of us isn't going to come back.' That's what she said." Britney sobbed for a few minutes more. "And the whole car ride up, I knew she was right, but I was afraid to say anything about it."

"She was wrong. Britney, she was wrong. You have to remember that. And maybe whoever is doing this knows that too, but you can't let them beat you. Okay? You can't let them destroy you."

He was saying all the right things. She held on to him as though he were the only thing holding her up.

When he awkwardly tried to untangle himself from her, she didn't want to let him go. She laced her fingers through his. She felt bad about her life. She felt bad for Melissa. She felt bad for Adam.

But she was so glad he was here next to her. Holding her hand. Sitting close to her. It seemed like the most natural thing in the world.

His thumb meandered slowly along the back of her hand. It felt nice. She squeezed briefly, a little pulse of encouragement.

She couldn't tell if she was sad anymore.

His face was so open, so unguarded when he finally looked at her. The two of them gazed into each other's eyes, neither sure of what to do next. She wanted to kiss him. It was a terrible thing to want to do, an unforgivable betrayal of Ricky and, even more, of Melissa, but she wanted it anyway.

"We shouldn't be doing this," she said.

"I know."

He crinkled his eyes like he was looking through her, deep into her secret self.

She couldn't hold back any longer. She pulled him toward her and hugged him. She kissed him.

Then, falling back on the bed, she kissed him again.

He held her tight. He buried his head in her chest.

"I can't believe it," she heard him say. "I've wanted this since I can remember. My whole life." The words tingled down her spine. She'd never felt such a strong desire.

He was the one doing the kissing now. Her eyelid, her ear, her nose, her neck. His tears covered her face.

"I'm such a horrible person," she said.

"You're not. Not at all," he said. "You're beautiful."

She pulled at the engagement ring on her finger, pried it off, and set it on the bedside table.

twenty-nine

In the dark of the Computer Rebooter, under a single clip lamp, Bobby shook and howled. The tears ran in torrents down his face. He wasn't playing games or tinkering with hard drives, not today.

He couldn't get that last conversation with Melissa out of his head. There was something about Adam Saft that disturbed him. Why did Adam know so much about that gun? Why had he been so opposed to telling Mr. Johnson that one of his guns had been stolen? He remembered the comment Adam had made after catching Bobby watching over Britney: "You're lucky I didn't go grab one of Mr. Johnson's guns and shoot you with it."

A quick Google search of Adam's name garnered forty-two hits.

Nineteen of them were for articles covering Adam's high school golf team in the *Manchester Herald*—games won and lost, points scored, etc. These weren't of any interest to Bobby.

Six were articles Adam himself had written for the JFK High School paper, *The Discovery,* about things like the controversy over the installation of Coke machines in the hallways, the congestion problems in the school parking lot, and the debate team's success in the state competition. They weren't terribly well written, Bobby noted, and Adam seemed to have been given all the worst assignments.

Most of the other hits came from a blog called Kissing the Wind. It belonged to some guy named Toby Richards, a friend of Adam's from New Hampshire.

Bobby read these in order, and at first, they consisted of the usual gossip and complaints about school. Typical stuff about which girls were cute and whether they would smile at you in the halls. Rankings of teachers based on the amount of homework they gave multiplied by how cool they were. Anecdotes about parties and stupid things Toby and Adam got up to over the weekend. As they went on, though, the entries began to change; in August of the year before, a rift began to develop between Toby and Adam:

Adam hasn't talked to me in a week. He got pissed at me because I told him it wasn't a big deal, everybody's parents get divorced nowadays. My parents are divorced. I said, he'll get used to it, but he doesn't believe me. It's almost like he's looking for an excuse to feel sorry for himself.

Throughout the semester, the problems between them grew:

The other day, Adam said to me, "People are mean. Everybody's just so cruel to each other. It almost makes you think it's not worth trying to be nice." I couldn't believe it. Or, actually, I could. He used to be one of the nicest guys in school, but now that he's started hanging out with Fisher Pomerantz and Hal Struthers, he's become almost as big of an asshole as they are. All they do is try and pick up girls—not even girls they like. It's like they're just trying to prove they can do it. When he's with them, Adam gets this look on his face like he thinks he's the coolest thing on earth.

And then Adam started to get in real trouble:

Here's the deal—or at least Adam's version of it: Fisher and Hal sell stolen fuzz busters and car radios. He doesn't completely know how it all works, but he says that they told him they'd give him a cut if he joined them. I don't know what he thinks. It's not like those guys are going to stick up for him. Their parents are powerful people, and his aren't. If he gets arrested, he's screwed.

So on Saturday, Adam was arrested for breaking into a car. He was trying to steal a fuzz buster. I could have told him this would happen.

Adam says Fisher and Hal set him up. He says that the whole stolen goods business was an elaborate joke, that they tricked him into doing it and then they made sure he got caught. He wanted me to help him get back at them, but I flat-out refused. I'm not even sure I believe him about them setting him up. He's really disturbed. He's been doing drugs—I know, because I smelled pot smoke on his clothes after lunch hour on Monday—and his favorite phrase now is "So-and-so (insert any random person's name here) deserves to die." He says this with a big grin on his face, so I can't tell how much he's joking, but still, it's spooky.

This went on for almost a month. Each entry would detail more and more of the odd things Adam was doing: skipping school, picking fights with kids who were smaller than him, whispering about setting Fisher's house on fire. It all culminated in Adam being kicked out of school:

He had a deer-hunting rifle in his locker, and they think he was planning to use it. If he was, it's news to me, but I still hope nobody wants me to talk to them about it. I wouldn't know what to say. He claims he had it because he was going to go hunting, but I've never known him to be much of a hunter, and the way he's been acting lately, I wouldn't put it past him to use it on people. I want to believe that underneath the bitterness and anger at all the crappy things that have happened to him in the past few months, he's still the same great guy he always was. But I just don't know.

There were links to newspaper stories from all over the state describing the incident at the school. It turned out that Adam's notebooks were full of doodles of skulls and pentagrams and stuff like that.

This wasn't the Adam that Bobby knew. He wondered which was the real one.

A later blog entry mentioned that Adam was being sent to Wisconsin to "give him the space to get his head screwed on straight."

He's going to be staying with some friend of his father's and he's really pissed off about the whole thing. The problem is the guy's daughter. Adam really hates her. Then again, since his parents separated, it seems like Adam hates all girls.

Bobby couldn't read any more of this. He was too angry.

He e-mailed the link to Detective Russell.

Then he clicked out of Explorer and tried to calm himself down by killing monsters until three in the morning.

thirty

She didn't hear him knock.

She didn't even hear him talking to her, not the first time. Or the second or third time.

It wasn't until her father was screaming at her—screaming like she'd never heard him scream, shouting, "What the hell's going on in here! Britney! Get up now! You don't have any idea how much trouble you're in!"—that she really woke up.

But oh, did she ever wake up then.

She bolted upright in the bed. Her eyes wild, her hair a frenzied mess of tangles, she barked, "What kind of trouble? Who's here? What's happening?" Then she realized where she was and what her father was looking at. She was naked and beside her, his body twisted around hers, Adam was naked too. She reached for something to cover herself with, but she couldn't find anything—the covers must have fallen to the floor in the night. There was nowhere to hide.

As she flung herself from the bed and scrambled for the sheet bunched up on the ground, she immediately jumped into have-mercy mode. "I'm sorry," she said. "I'm sorry, I'm sorry, I'm sorry."

Adam was already jumping into his jeans. He raced toward the door, but Britney's father caught him by the arm.

"Don't think your parents aren't going to hear about this, Adam," he said. "I might just have to ship you home."

Adam writhed and cringed. He seemed terribly afraid of this idea. "Please, don't do that," he said. "Please, please . . . they'll kill me. There's no way. . . . I can't go back there."

"Well, we're going to discuss it. After the funeral. All three of us are going to have a long talk and figure out what to do about this." He released Adam's elbow and Adam flew down the stairs.

Then he was back to Britney.

"Sorry won't cut it, Brit."

"Dad—"

"Don't Dad me." He was still in his bathrobe, a thick maroon terry cloth gown that Britney had bought him for his birthday last year.

"Dad—"

"You really—you think you can get away with anything, don't you? Well, I'll tell you right now, you can't. Not in this house. I see more than you think I do."

His face was beet red. Britney stared at him, afraid of what he might say next.

"And I don't like it," he finally said.

She wanted to tell him that he had no right to judge her, that her body belonged to her, not to him, that given the circumstances, what she and Adam had done the night before was more mature and less selfish and more beautiful than drowning their sorrow in a whiskey bottle like he had. She wanted to tell him so many things, but she couldn't, not like this.

"Just let me get dressed, Dad, okay?" she screamed. "Then you can yell at me all you want."

He took a deep breath, holding it so long that Britney thought he might explode. He exhaled with an unbelievable force and something softened in him.

"Okay," he said quietly. "I'll be downstairs in my office. Waiting."

Before shutting the door, he gave her a long, pitying look. Or was it a tender look? It could have gone either way.

Taking deep breaths herself, Britney tried to calm down. She knew that beneath his anger, her father meant well. The murders and terror were having an effect on him, just like they were on her—just like they were on everybody. After she dressed, she'd go down and talk to him and try to make sure he knew how contrite she was.

She hoped it wouldn't take long. She didn't want to miss Melissa's funeral, which was supposed to start in barely an hour. Her hope had been to go with Adam, or with her father, or both of them, so she'd have some support during what she knew would be an emotionally wrenching experience.

Now that would be too uncomfortable. She called Erin and explained how anxious she was.

"Why don't you call Troy?" said Erin. "I'm sure he'd be willing to go with you."

"You wouldn't mind?"

"Are you kidding? It's crazy what's going on. I'm scared out of my wits and I don't even know these people. I can only imagine what you must be feeling."

When she spoke to Troy, he said, "Listen, you know what, I'll do even better than that. I'll get all the guys together. Anybody who wants to get to you will have to go through us first."

Reminding him that she really just needed moral support to get through the funeral, she made a plan for him to pick her up; she'd wait in front of her house.

Then she went downstairs to have that dreaded talk with her dad.

thirty-one

There weren't enough Jewish people living in Madison for them to have a cemetery of their own, so the memorial service for Melissa and Karl was held at the Mendota Funeral Home, housed inside the Mendota cemetery, which kept a rabbi on staff.

Detective Tara Russell stood in the shadows near the back door of the richly wooded room and watched the congregants closely. The service was small and sparsely attended, mostly by friends of David and Margie Brown, Melissa's parents. Tara was sure that the killer would show up to witness the pain he'd caused. That was why she was there.

The Browns had waited until they were in their mid-thirties to have children; their friends were middle-aged, couples mostly, the men in ill-fitting, worn suits, the women in heavy dark skirts, big brooches pinned to their blouses. They didn't look like the killing sort—more the NPR-listening, Indian-food-eating sort. University types.

Karl didn't seem to have any friends. Detective Russell figured that most of the people he'd wasted his life with weren't the type to notice he was gone.

For a long time, she feared that none of Melissa's friends would show up either. Britney was nowhere to be found. Bobby and Adam both arrived late. They came in separately, within minutes of each other. Picking yarmulkes out of the little wicker basket by the entrance, they gave each other suspicious looks and found seats in pews on opposite sides of the room.

She'd spent the morning reading through the blog Bobby had sent her. Now that she knew what she was dealing with, she was surer than ever of her instincts about Adam. She'd even faxed the Manchester, New Hampshire, police force and asked for any records they had on him, but they told her they probably wouldn't be able to get back to her for several days. Their budget had been cut and they were understaffed. In the meantime, she hoped to find out all she could.

When Britney did arrive, the service was almost over. She brought an escort with her: a group of six guys from the hockey team. They hadn't dressed for the occasion. Instead of the appropriate mourning clothes, they were garbed in sweat clothes and cross-trainers, backward baseball caps.

Tara noticed that Britney was especially nervous. Every few minutes, she glanced around like she thought someone was out to get her. She and her entourage sat in the back row, and throughout the service, she hardly moved. She was so still that she looked like a wax statue of herself.

She felt bad for the girl. To have survived the loss of her mother only to watch all her friends die away—it was hard to fathom how much strength it must take to endure this. If she could get through the coming months, and the bleakness she would feel as she tried to come to grips with everything that had just happened in her life, she might turn out okay, but the interim would be rough.

Thinking it might help Britney feel more secure, Tara walked a few paces up the aisle and waved at her. She wanted to say, "I'm here and you're safe," but the service was in progress, and this was impossible. She hoped that just seeing her would be enough for Britney.

As the service progressed, Tara tried to put the pieces she had together. The pace of the killings was accelerating, and she knew she had to crack the case soon if she wanted to avert any further horror. Karl had been involved. She was sure of that. At this very moment, the guys from the lab were going over his red Ford pickup, and she was sure they'd find something linking it to Ricky Piekowski's death. But why had Karl been killed? And how had he gotten that gun? He must have been working with someone—either Ed Johnson or Adam Saft—but which one, and what had gone wrong to spur whoever it was to kill him? If there was only some way for her to get into the Johnson house and see what she could find. The reception was held at the Brown residence, and as soon as she had the opportunity, Tara pulled Britney away from her cohort of hockey jocks.

"I just wanted to see how you're holding up," she said.

"I'm fine," Britney said. She looked uncomfortable. She kept looking over at her bodyguards as though they were some sort of magical bubble outside of which she couldn't breathe. Detective Russell noticed that today Britney wasn't wearing the engagement ring Ricky had given her.

They were standing near the small circular table in the corner of the living room, which had been laid out with a spread of veggies and dip, bagels and lox, and oversized chocolate chip cookies. The whole house was markedly cleaner than it had been when she had spoken with Melissa; the piles of books and papers had been stashed away somewhere. A steady stream of guests made their way past the table, piling food onto the tiny plastic plates that had been provided for them. They all talked about the same thing: how frightening it was to think that whoever had done this was still at large and would probably strike again.

"Hey, where's your dad? I figured I'd see him here," she asked.

Britney shot her a look—a darting, fleeting look of paranoia.

"I don't know," she said. "He was running late. He told me to leave without him."

The defensiveness and fear in her voice was icy thick. It made Tara wonder if Britney had lost faith in her ability to crack the case.

"I know you don't think I'm doing enough," she said, putting her arm around Britney's shoulders and walking her away toward the stairs, where, she thought, they might be able to carve out some privacy, "but these things take time. I've got some leads now, and if they pan out—"

"Hey, yo, Britney—" One of the hockey players, a beefy guy with long slicked-back blond hair had noticed the two of them talking. "If you can't see me, I can't see you."

Sighing, Britney said, "It's okay. She's a cop."

The guy smirked.

"This is Troy," Britney said. Then, as though this clarified something important, "He's giving me moral support."

"And his friends?"

"Them too."

Tara made a motion as though she were tipping a cap at Troy, dismissing him. She walked Britney away from the crowd, and the two of them sat partway up the staircase. From here, they could speak in semi-privacy.

They could also see the whole room through the wooden banister rods, and as Tara told Britney the few things she could about the case, she surveyed the activity below them.

The hockey players were gorging themselves, taking three or four plates apiece from the table and piling them high with food. The detective worried that they might start a food fight, throw smoked salmon at the walls just to see if it would stick, or pull any of a myriad of other stupid pranks.

Bobby sulked against the wall near the front door, as though he were sullenly guarding it. His eyes took in everything, but he was paying special attention to Britney and Adam, glancing back and forth between them.

Adam was extremely nervous. He tried to hide it, to blend in with the other mourners, but he couldn't sit still. He incessantly slicked his hands through the part in his hair and wandered across the room every few minutes, in a way that seemed meant to be inconspicuous, to check on Britney's whereabouts.

The blog Bobby had sent her had mentioned that Adam despised Britney; this was as good a place to start as any. "So, listen, I thought you might be able to tell me a little about Adam. What's your relationship like with him?" she asked Britney.

"Why?" There was that snappish fearful tone again. The girl was incredibly defensive today.

"Well, I'm curious. He seems like an okay kid. But I don't know much about him. You see him every day. What can you tell me? I mean, I know his parents are splitting up, but how does that affect his moods? Is he angry a lot around the house?"

Britney waffled back and forth on this one. She talked about how annoying Adam could be, and then in the next breath, she said he was charming, "a gentleman," "the kind of guy that you have a hard time believing exists."

Tara took notes as she listened.

"Do you know if he knew Karl Brown at all?"

"I don't kn—"

A sudden commotion from the other side of the room stopped their conversation short. The hockey players were pushing through the adults and forming in a loose circle.

It was hard to see who they had in the center of the ring, but Tara had a good guess: Bobby and Adam. The rancor she'd sensed earlier between them had been palpable and she couldn't imagine them lasting long in the same room together without a confrontation.

This was confirmed by Adam's voice, singing out bitterly, "I don't need to listen to this stuff from you, Bobby, you perv!"

And Bobby's voice coming right back at him: "Why not? If it's true! Why not? Unless you're hiding something. Are you? Huh? What are you hiding?"

"You're crazy."

"Oh, I'm crazy now, huh? I'm the one who's crazy! Why don't you tell her what happened in New Hampshire?! Huh? Why don't you tell her what you said about her to your friend Toby Richards?"

"You don't know anything about it, Bobby! You're the one crawling around in the dark, spying on her all the time!"

There was a surge of noise as Bobby took a swing at Adam.

"You want to go? I'll go with you," said Adam.

The hockey players began chanting, "Fight. Fight. Fight."

"Aren't you going to stop them?" asked Britney, alarmed. She was holding her head in her hands as though somehow she could block the whole thing out.

Tara slowly stood up and began to make her way toward the excitement. She wanted to let the boys go for a while in hopes that in the heat of passion, one of them would say something incriminating.

"You think you can take me, you freaking perv?" Adam taunted.

A snorting and spitting sound came from the circle, and there was a loud chorus of grunts from the hockey players.

The other adults in the room were doing what they could. Melissa's mother was pleading, "Bobby, please, whatever this is about, let it go. Remember what you're here for. Don't you think Melissa would be unhappy to see you fighting like this?" A few of the men tried to break through and manually restrain the boys, but the hockey players wouldn't let them in.

Once she saw the first fist rise above the crowd, Tara moved faster. She pulled a pair of handcuffs off her belt. Shouting, "Police officer—break it up, break it up," she pushed through the throng and into the circle. She made sure that the first wrist she grabbed belonged to Adam.

While she wrangled him to the ground, the hockey players tried to hold down Bobby. He fought and squirmed, and finally he kicked one of them in the shin, wriggling away somehow and slamming out of the house.

Adam flailed and made it difficult for her to cuff him.

"Come on," he said. "Bobby started it! He's the one you should be arresting."

"You scared?" she said, eliciting a round of laughter from the hockey guys.

She called in some backup.

She explained what was going to happen to him. "I'm not going to arrest you for assault—though I could—I'm arresting you for disorderly conduct. You know the drill already, don't you, Adam? Who knows, if you behave yourself, they might let you go on your own recognizance."

She hoped that they'd hold him longer than that. If she

could search the house while he was locked up and, with any luck, pick up enough evidence to book him for the larger crimes she suspected him of, that would be great.

Once the officers showed up to take Adam away, Tara talked to Melissa's parents for a while. They were in shock. The reception was ruined. Most of the guests were leaving. And some of their stuff had been destroyed in the scuffle, most notably the framed Matisse print that they'd received as a wedding gift from David Brown's parents.

Explaining the procedure for filing a complaint and calming them down as well as she could, Detective Russell left them to clean up the mess.

She found Britney sitting on the stairs, right where she'd left her. Her head was in her hands. The hockey players were situated in a protective circle around her.

"Why'd you arrest Adam?" Britney asked.

The hockey players were as eager for Detective Russell's answer as Britney.

They all had the same question. "What's up with him?" "Do you think he's the one who's been doing all this stuff?" "Is he the killer?"

Everyone in the room was anxiously listening. She didn't want to give anything away. "They're both in trouble. Adam just happens to be the one I caught. I'll deal with Bobby later. Listen, Britney, let me give you a ride home, what do you say?" When Britney looked apprehensive, the detective nodded at the hockey players and said, "Come on, Britney, Who do you think you're safer with, them or me?"

thirty-two

The fact that this was her father hadn't sunk in yet. She understood it intellectually. She recognized his blue slacks and the black tie with the textured black stripes. She recognized his large hands, though the way they cradled the shotgun—one hand on the barrel, thumb looped around the trigger, the other clenched tightly around the base of the shoulder rest—was grotesque, unnatural, hard for her to fully comprehend at the moment.

Britney shrieked.

She shrieked and shrieked. She couldn't stop.

It felt like someone had grabbed her by the neck and was squeezing with all his might, holding her head in place so that no matter how much she wanted to turn away, she had to look.

Right now, all she was able to register was the gore. The shelf behind his desk that contained his old law school books, slick with blood. The metal balance-weighted sculpture, that airplane he liked to spin while he thought over his cases, tipped off the stand now, wrapped in deep crimson ribbons of what could only be brains. The shards of bone glued to his framed diploma.

Most of all she saw his head, or what was left of it, larger than life, his right eye dangling from a shattered socket, his skull sheared in half, leaking thick globular blood, his jaw hanging slack from one hinge.

Detective Russell was holding her, an arm around her shoulders, a hand softly to her head. Britney sank into her embrace. That felt nice. A relief, just for a moment, from holding herself up. Her shrieks slowly evolved into sobs.

"Don't look, Britney. Just don't look. Come on. Let's go into the other room. Here . . . let's . . . yeah . . . this way."

The detective led her, almost carried her, out of the den. They wove through the hallway past the downstairs bathroom. Britney let herself be directed.

"Sit now. Yes. It's okay."

But it wasn't okay, and hearing the detective say those words, Britney felt another surge of emotion well up in her. She buried her head. She ached with emptiness.

The detective was brushing the hair out of her face, rubbing her back. "It's okay. I'm here."

Everything moved so slowly. Each breath she took lasted an eternity. And every time she felt like she was returning from the ocean in which she was drowning, a riptide reared up and dragged her back into the deep.

"We need to find someplace for you to go."

Britney couldn't respond.

"Somewhere safe. I need you to think, Britney. Where could you go?"

It was all she could do to listen.

"You could come to my house. I've got an extra bedroom. It's small. There's only a futon, but it's okay. What do you think of that, Britney?"

Britney shook her head no. Thinking was good. Thinking helped plug up the emotions and push them back.

"Are you sure? It would be like we were having a slumber party. How's that sound?"

"I want to stay—" It was a struggle to speak. Her voice broke as she got to the end of her sentence, and the final word was overrun by more tears. "—here."

"I don't think you should do that."

Britney had no answer. Where she went, what she did, even who she was, none of this seemed important at the moment.

"What do you say, Britney? Will you stay at my place for a while—until we find somewhere safe for you to go?"

"I guess," said Britney with a noncommittal shrug. She couldn't think of anything better.

"I promise it'll be fine," said the detective after a few more minutes of holding her while she cried. When she finally stood up, she said, "I need to work now. I need to deal with . . . the other room."

The idea of being alone was horrifying. "Don't go."

"I'll be right here, just ten feet away, okay? When the other officers get here, maybe we can find someone to sit with you. Can you be strong for twenty minutes or so?"

Britney nodded, and the detective walked away, leaving her alone. Britney gazed out the window. The weather seemed to be mocking her—six straight days of sunshine and rising temperatures. Today it was almost fifty. Beautiful weather. The kind of weather that made you feel like you were waking up from a deep hibernation and reentering a world that you thought had died for good. It made her angry. How could the world decide to be so sunny when her house had suddenly become so dark?

She gradually realized that her cell was chiming. The screen said "unknown caller." She answered it anyway.

"Britney!" It was Bobby Plumley. He was out of breath.

"What do you want?"

"I need to see you."

"I don't have time for—"

"Don't hang up, don't hang up! I need to see you as soon as humanly possible."

"Why?"

"Where are you? Are you at home?"

"Yeah."

"Well, that's no good. You have to leave. You can't stay there."

He sounded almost as hysterical as she felt.

"You know what? I'm glad you called. I've got that police officer right here. You're going to be arrested, Bobby."

"I—you've really got to get out of there. It's really danger-ous. I'm serious, Britney. I know what's been going on. I've fig-ured it out. I know who's been killing everybody."

Her adrenaline surged.

"Who?"

"I need you to meet me at the Sanctuary. Will you come? Please? Okay?"

She thought for a moment. She didn't trust him.

"I guess so, sure," she said finally.

"As soon as you can. It's humongously important."

She had to go. She had to find out what Bobby knew. She was scared of him, but not as scared as she was of the uncer-tainty and torture that was overwhelming her. Her body wouldn't stop shaking; it was as though all her cells had decided to riot and they were slam dancing chaotically against one another.

She could hear the detective rummaging around behind the closed door of her father's den. She didn't want to knock on the door; she didn't want to think about what she was doing. The detective would try to persuade her to stay where she was—especially if she knew that Britney was going to meet Bobby Plumley.

Tiptoeing into the kitchen, she found a large knife and, wrapping it in paper towels so it wouldn't cut her, she placed it inside Ricky's letter jacket. Better safe than sorry, she thought. Bobby was dangerous.

Then she stealthily slipped out the back door and ran to her car, glancing behind her side to side in all directions the whole time, hoping to get away before the detective noticed and before the other cops arrived.

She just missed them. As she drove down Pine Crest toward Washington Avenue, the police cars whizzed past in the opposite direction, their sirens wailing. She could only hope that none of the cops recognized her.

thirty-three

As forensics trooped back and forth from their van to the den where Ed Johnson's body was, Tara snooped around.

She went through Ed Johnson's bedroom first. It was fastidiously clean, almost barren. A bed, a dresser on which rested a dish overflowing with quarters, all lined up as though ready to be slid into rolls, a tie rack, and a single straight-back chair. Nothing on the walls. Nothing was out of place.

The only thing that she found odd at all was that the photo of his wife, Jan, in her wedding dress had been tipped face-down. But even this had been done in a conscientious manner. It was carefully lined up so that the edges of the frame were in parallel lines with the edges of the dresser.

If he'd been suicidal, he'd still had the wits to keep everything in his bedroom in order.

What troubled her was that there wasn't a note. It made her wonder if he'd done this in a rush of irrational feeling.

When she was done in Ed Johnson's room, she noticed that Britney's door was slightly ajar, so she stepped inside to have a look.

The closet was a real teenage mess. So many clothes and whatever else—old notebooks, paperback books, a see-through umbrella with balloons painted onto it, a tattered stuffed frog, all kinds of stuff—that it was like a solid, waist-high wall. The boudoir was overflowing with baubles, silver bracelets, neck-laces, hair-care products. Photos cut from magazines and news-papers of hunky movie stars and singers were taped to the large round mirror.

The bed was a knot of sheets and blankets, a patchwork quilt braided through the stream of other coverings. Just visible under-neath this were the tongue of a tube sock, the strap of a bra.

Tara began to notice other things that she'd overlooked at first.

The boys' New Balance running shoes, much too big for Britney's small feet, one sticking out from under the bed, the other off in the corner as though it had been thrown there.

On the floor was a crumpled pair of blue-and-white-striped boxer shorts.

"Are you looking for something specific?"

It was Adam Saft, home from the police station. He leaned against the doorway, watching her with a mixture of anger, fear, and curiosity on his face.

"How'd you get in here? This is a crime scene!"

"I don't know," he said. "The door was open."

She didn't push it. He was a prime suspect, and now that she had him in her sights, she didn't want to let him go. Holding up the boxers, she asked him, "Do you know who these belong to?"

"Uh . . ." He blushed.

"They're yours, aren't they?"

"Can I plead the fifth?" He let out a little smirk, as though he was proud of himself, but it quickly faded.

"First Melissa, now Britney—you're a real ladies' man, Adam. And you don't seem all that upset about what's happened downstairs."

"I don't know what happened," he said. "Nobody will tell me."

"It looks like Mr. Johnson has killed himself."

She probed his face for a reaction. He blanched and tensed up, his eyes moving off to someplace far away, and she couldn't read his expression.

"You don't have any idea why, do you?"

"Not exactly."

"What's that mean?"

He hemmed and hawed like he was deliberating with himself about how much information it was safe to reveal.

Tara leaned back onto her shoulders on the bed. "Come sit next to me." She patted the spot next to her invitingly.

Reluctantly, he did as she asked. He wouldn't look at her.

"So? Something must have happened. Why don't you tell me?"

"Well . . ." He squirmed uncomfortably. "We got busted, big

time. And he threatened to send me home." He couldn't hide the bitterness in his voice.

"Did that piss you off?"

She could tell he felt trapped. He was patting an anxious rhythm on his legs.

"Look, what do you want from me?"

"I'm just curious, Adam. Is there some reason you wouldn't want to go home?"

Suddenly putting the implications together, he turned on her. "You think I killed him, don't you?!"

"Did I say that?"

"No, but—"

"Then where'd you get that idea?"

He was looking around now. Sizing up an escape route, she thought.

Changing tactics, she asked, "How well did you know Karl Brown?"

"I didn't know him at all!" Adam looked horrified; his voice had taken on a pleading tone. "He and Mr. Johnson were tight."

Detective Russell frowned. "You never even met him once?"

"No!"

A soft rapping at the door interrupted them, and one of the guys from forensics stuck his head in. "We've found something on Ed Johnson's computer that you might want to look at," he said.

She told Adam to stay right where he was and stepped outside, shutting the door behind her.

thirty-four

To: Edward Johnson (ejohnson@johnsoncrimdef.com)

From: Melissa Brown (sillyrabbit@plumley.com)

Re: Britney

Dear Mr. Johnson,

Thanks for all the stuff you did for Karl during the past few years. We Browns—I mean my parents mostly—don't really express ourselves very well, but we all really appreciate how hard you worked for him and all the ways you tried to protect him. Without you, he'd probably still be in jail.

That's not why I'm writing you, though. There are a few things that have been nagging at me.

First, did Karl ever meet Britney's mother? I know she had her problems and mostly hid away when other people came around, but the few times I got to talk to her, she seemed very compassionate—like she had a sixth sense or something and could tell what you were thinking and feeling just by looking at you. I wonder what she would have thought of Karl. Do you know? Could you tell me?

Second—and I don't know how much of this you already know, but I'm going to tell you anyway—I'm really worried about Britney.

Before she started dating Ricky and hanging out with that new crowd of hers, she used to tell me things. Did you know that she feels responsible for what happened to her mother? Not like guilty for still being alive responsible, either. She feels really responsible. Like it was all her fault. I don't know what happened on that rafting trip, but she was convinced that if she hadn't been there, her mother would still be alive.

I keep thinking back to the time she tried to kill herself after her mom died. She went out to this favorite spot of ours. We call it the Sanctuary because nobody really knows about it but us, and whenever we go there, it feels sort of holy. She ran a hose from the exhaust of her car into the driver's side window and locked herself in. If Bobby Plumley hadn't happened to show up, she probably wouldn't be here today.

After that, Bobby and I took turns watching her, following her around like babysitters to make sure she didn't do anything drastic.

And then she hooked up with Ricky and everything seemed to be getting better. She was happy finally.

She made me swear not to tell you any of this. She didn't want you to feel more burdened than you already do. I feel like I have to, though.

I'm afraid she's going to try it again.

Ricky's dead. Karl's dead. Everyone seems to be dying and Britney is acting weird again. She's so fragile. And I know she thinks these deaths are all her fault—just like she did about her mother. Has she talked about any of this with you?

You probably think it's weird that I'm writing all this in an e-mail, but like I said, I'm really worried about Britney. I didn't want to wait until we had a time to meet to tell you about it.

There's one more thing. I found some really disturbing things while I was cleaning out Karl's room. Is there somewhere we can get together and talk that Britney wouldn't see us so I can show them to you? The things I found really spooked me.

Melissa

"Does Britney know you found this?" asked Detective Russell.

The officer shook his head. "I haven't even seen her."

"She's downstairs in the living room."

"Um—no, she's not."

Detective Russell was alarmed. She silently cursed herself for letting Britney out of her sight. "She's not?"

Shaking his head again, the officer said, "Sorry." Then, moving on, he said, "Listen, there's one more thing. We've heard back on the prints from the gun."

"And?"

He checked his notes. "Three sets: Ed Johnson, Adam Saft, and a partial we couldn't identify."

"Thanks." She nodded toward the closed door behind her. "I've got Adam Saft right here. I'll keep an eye on him. I want you to search the house. We've got to find Britney before she does something to herself!"

thirty-five

Adam could hear their muffled voices on the other side of the door, but he couldn't make out what they were saying. He was worried they might be talking about him. He'd come to Madison to get away from trouble, but now he was afraid he might be in even more trouble than he'd gotten himself into in New Hampshire.

When the detective returned to the room, she was even less friendly than when she'd left. Her stare disturbed him. It was so accusatory.

"What happened?" he asked.

"Have you ever heard of a place called the Sanctuary?"

"Melissa took me there once. Why?" Adam ran his fingers through the part in his hair over and over, as though he were trying to pull the hair right out.

"Where is it?"

"It's a park. Me-something. Some Indian name."

"Menominee Park?"

"Yeah, that's it."

The detective stuck her head out the door and shouted down the hallway. "Have you found her yet?"

A voice carried up the stairs. "Negative. We've covered the whole property. She's not here."

Adam frantically asked what was going on, but the detective ignored him.

"You're positive?" she called out to the officer down the stairs.

"We can keep searching if you want."

"Yeah, do that." Turning to Adam, she said, "Come on, let's go."

"What's going on?" Adam asked, but she was already out the door, scrambling into her jacket. He had no choice but to follow her.

They raced to Detective Russell's car. As soon as she had the ignition going, Detective Russell cracked the window and, taking the wad of gum out of her mouth, lit a cigarette.

"At least tell me where we're going," said Adam.

"We're going to Menominee Park to find Britney," snapped the detective.

"What happened? Is she okay?"

"That's what we're going to find out."

Hitting a button on the dashboard, the detective squealed the cruiser out of the driveway and splashed through the puddles that the melting ice had left in the street. The siren shrieked and they chased off toward the park.

Adam was tense. His fear for Britney's safety was overwhelming.

"Why won't you tell me what's going on?" he asked.

She just glared at him—she seemed tense and nervous too—and he shrank into his seat. It was no use; she wasn't going to tell him anything.

He felt lucky to be up front for once. Every time he'd been in a police car before—just this morning had been the most recent—he'd been in the back, behind the bulletproof glass partition, sitting awkwardly on his cuffed hands, his back pressing into the hard plastic seat. It was nicer up front with handles on the door and plush vinyl cushioning behind him.

"So, we got this call, Adam," she said. Her eyes were fixed on the road. Something in her tone filled him with dread.

"Yeah?"

"From the guys in forensics."

"Okay—"

"And they . . . The gun that Britney's father shot himself with. Have you ever seen that gun before, Adam?"

Heat rushed to Adam's face and he began to sweat.

"Uh—I don't know. I'd have to look at it."

"So you might have."

He shrugged. He didn't want to tell her anything he didn't have to.

"What would you say if I told you we found your prints on it, Adam?"

"I'd say—wait, I thought you said he killed himself?"

"I said it *looked* like he killed himself."

"So, what? You think *I* killed him?!"

"Why don't you tell me why your prints might be on that gun, Adam," she said, with the smallest of glances in his direction.

He couldn't speak as fast as he was thinking. "We both like to hunt. A while ago, right when I got to town, he was showing me his gun because we both liked to hunt and he wanted to show me his gun." The panic he felt was like a nutcracker chomping down on his temples. "And so I held it and sighted it up and stuff to get the feel of it. I don't even know where he kept it. I swear." He could hear his voice as he spoke, and it didn't sound convincing. The more afraid he got, the shriller he became.

The detective's cheeks puckered in on themselves as she took a long drag on her cigarette, and then she said, "Tell me about New Hampshire, Adam."

It was hopeless. He felt trapped. He wished she would stop saying his name after every sentence.

"I was having a hard time."

Outside, the city streamed past, the coffee shops and boutiques and used bookstores and ramshackle wooden houses where the college students lived. The weather had turned. People were everywhere, strolling around like they'd just woken up from a hundred-year sleep to discover, to their amazement, that the world was still beautiful. Adam imagined what it would be like never to be able to walk like that again. He suddenly wanted to feel the wind on his face.

"Can I roll down the window?" he asked.

"No."

The detective lit another cigarette.

"You had some trouble with guns in New Hampshire too, didn't you?"

"It was in my car!" he pleaded. "I was going to go hunting after school! God! I didn't do anything wrong." He picked at the chipped chrome around the handle of the car door.

The police radio growled, and Detective Russell answered it.

"Tara?"

"You've got me; what's the news?"

"We've got test results on your 187. His hands are clean."

"What's that mean?" Adam asked once she hung up.

She looked him dead in the eye and said, "That means Britney's dad didn't pull the trigger. There was no residue on his hands."

The street widened into four lanes, and the houses started to become interspersed with thick clusters of trees. They passed a wooden sign that said something Park, but it went by so fast that Adam couldn't read it. With the snowbanks dwindling, everything looked slightly different. He couldn't remember if this was the same place.

When they veered into the parking lot, he felt another shudder of dread. Up ahead of them was Britney's yellow VW Bug. And parked right next to it was Bobby's red pickup.

thirty-six

Adam's fear for his own safety had vanished as soon as he'd seen Bobby's truck next to Britney's car. He was too worried about her, worried for her life, to think of himself.

He and the detective splashed through the icy puddles in the parking lot toward the vehicles. No one was there, but soggy footprints in the slush and gravel pointed into the winding pathways of the park.

"This way," shouted Adam.

They raced through the trees, brushing roughly past wet shrubs, kicking and stomping through the tangle of saplings that the melting snow had revealed.

When they got to the bench, they wheeled and stopped. The waterlogged footprints they were following led directly onto the lake. Fifty feet out or so, they stopped at a partially submerged brick-red ice-fishing shack, which had begun to tip through the ice toward one corner.

"Wait," said the detective, "we have to find another way. It's not safe."

But Adam was already charging ahead. As he jumped onto the ice, he heard a loud popping sound below him, then a series of creaks and full-bellied groans from the ice adjusting to his weight.

Despite her best judgment, Detective Russell followed him.

Striding with great leaps, slipping and sliding, each step holding the possibility of breaking through, they rushed to the ice-fishing shack.

There was shouting coming from inside. A male voice. Bobby Plumley. "Help me," he screamed. "Somebody, help me!"

Where was Britney? Why wasn't she shouting too?

Adam got there first and he tried to pull the door open, but it was locked from the inside. From the way the door twisted, he could see that the lock was flimsy, nothing more than a hook through a metal loop.

"Where's Britney?" Adam yelled. "Open the door, Bobby."

"I can't reach it. I'm stuck," came the voice from inside.

"Bobby, let me in!" Adam pulled with all his might. With every yank, the shack rattled. Bobby was making a whole lot of noise, but he wasn't opening up.

Detective Russell pulled her baton out of her belt, and with great precision she wedged it under the lock and twisted, snapping the metal in two.

The door flew open.

The hole in the ice was huge. As the water had warmed, the area where the fishermen had drilled to drop their lines into had spread. Now it was almost as wide as the shack itself.

Bobby had fallen through. His flop of hair was partially wet; it hung down over his cheeks. He'd lost his glasses, and the spots on his nose where they normally rested looked waxy. His lips were blue. With one hand, he grasped onto the bench built into the far wall of the shack, and there was a dark division of color where his snowmobile suit was soaked through. His other hand held what looked like a bundled-up article of clothing, golden leather and deep red wool.

He flopped the bundle up out of the water at Adam. It was Ricky Piekowski's letter jacket. The one Britney never took off.

"I'm so cold." Bobby was shivering. His lower lip shook like it was surging with current. He was crying.

"Adam, help me," barked the detective. She had already scoped the shack out and was testing how tightly it was locked to the ice. On her directions, Adam braced his feet on the outer right edge of the door. She did the same on the left. They each took one of Bobby's arms and, using the shack itself for leverage, they swung him up out of the water.

"Where is she? What did you do with her?" Adam yelled.

Bobby's whole body shook and jittered.

"I w-w-was trying to save her." Stammering, he tried to make himself understood. "I was . . ."

As what had happened began to sink in, Adam began to feel dizzy, weak. He let go of Bobby and sank to his knees.

Bobby stared through bloodshot eyes at Adam.

"This is all your fault! You saw she was happy and . . . I tried to tell her, but she wou-wouldn't listen. She was upset. And . . . and . . . and . . ."

Suddenly Adam was on top of Bobby. He had him by the collar of his snowmobile suit. He shook him violently. He was shrieking, "You killed her! You killed her! You bastard!" The tears streamed down his face.

The detective was preoccupied by something on her hand. She studied her fingers, rubbed them together. She held her hand up to her face and smelled it. Pulling Adam off Bobby, she pointed to a spot nearby and said, "Stand there." Then she turned to Bobby. "What happened?"

"She took off running. I was scared. I remember what she was like right after her mother died. So I chased her and she ran faster and I almost caught her, but I slipped and fell on the ice and she ran into this shack and she sat on the bench. She was crying. We were both crying. She was writing something—here."

He dug in his pocket and pulled a crumpled, wet piece of loose-leaf paper out of it.

"I have it here. I grabbed it from her."

The detective grabbed the paper and smoothed it over her knee. Studying it with the same scrupulous attention she'd been giving to her hand.

"She wanted to kill herself. And I tried to hold her back.

I tried to pull her out toward the shore, but she fought with me and the ice cracked under us and she lunged up and locked the door and then she jumped, feet first, into the water. I couldn't hold on. I had her by the sleeve of her jacket, and it slipped off her in my hands. I saw her go under. She . . . I couldn't stop her."

"She's down there?" Adam shouted. "Then she might still be alive!" He darted for the hole in the ice, stripping off his jacket, ready to dive in and fish Britney out, but Detective Russell caught him by the waist and held him—kicking and screaming—back.

"It's too late," she said. "You can't save her."

He struggled against her, pried at her fingers and kicked at her shins, but her grip was tight and he couldn't get loose of her. Eventually, he sank to his knees and buried his head in his hands.

The detective was reading and reading the note Bobby had given her.

When Adam could speak again, he asked, "What's it say?"

She handed it over.

The paper had been soaked through and become translucent, but the words scrawled on it had been written in ballpoint pen. They were still clearly legible:

I've had enough. I'm through with all of you.

It wasn't signed.

"This isn't Britney's handwriting," he said "It's not Bobby's either, but it isn't Britney's."

"I saw her writing it! I pulled it right out of her hands!"

"Yeah, just like you saw me kill all those people. You're full of shit, Bobby."

Bobby lay limp on the ice, staring at the sky, as though out of sheer exhaustion. A wry smile cracked over his face.

Adam handed the note back to the detective. "Detective, this isn't her handwriting. I swear." She took it without even looking. She was still focused on the ice-fishing shack.

"We should get off this ice," she finally said. She carefully folded the note and put it in the pocket of her jacket.

"Come on, Bobby, I'll help you up."

She reached out and, taking Bobby by the wrists, pulled him to his feet. Then she turned his hands over and looked at his palms.

"That's what I thought," she said. "Bobby, you know when you fire a gun, the residue gets all over your hands. I'm going to have to place you under arrest."

Bobby squirmed; he kicked at her shins and twisted violently, but he couldn't break her grip. Finally he bit her, and as she reacted, he swung his elbow into her jaw.

He was off, racing toward the shore. The ice underneath him was popping and cracking.

The detective dashed after him and, struggling to his feet, Adam followed.

The melting ice was almost impossible to run on. There were thin spots everywhere, hidden by the slushy layer on top, and twice Adam's lunging foot fell through into the icy water. The detective and Bobby were having similar problems, but Bobby, with his head start, was gaining ground.

Digging his toes into the soft surface, Adam pushed to catch Bobby—he'd reached the shore. He had an exposed root in his hand and was struggling to pull himself up onto the land with it. Adam dove. He grabbed Bobby's boot, but Bobby twisted and kept climbing. The boot slid off into Adam's hand with such force that it threw him sprawling backward.

And Bobby was off again, on land now.

Adam was right behind him. When Bobby swung around the wooden bench, Adam jumped right over it and almost nabbed him, but Bobby grabbed a trunk and spun himself quickly in a new direction.

They chased through the trees.

They'd lost the detective.

Bobby kept weaving and dodging, gradually making his way toward the parking lot and his truck. When he hit the edge of the woods, he broke into a sprint.

Adam was losing ground. There was no way he'd catch him now.

Then, just as Bobby was about to reach his truck, the detective leapt out from behind Britney's VW Bug and grabbed him. She twisted his arm behind his back, lifting him almost off the ground.

"Bobby Plumley, I'm placing you under arrest," she said, "for the murders of Britney and Edward Johnson."

thirty-seven

THE MADISON CAPITAL TIMES

FEBRUARY 20

Early yesterday afternoon, a prime suspect in the recent string of grisly murders that have been tormenting the populace of Madison was taken into custody by the Madison Police Department. Robert Plumley, 18, of Madison, was arrested and charged with two counts of first-degree murder for the deaths of Mr. Edward Johnson and his daughter, Britney Johnson.

Detective Tara Russell of the MPD has told the *Capital Times* that within the next few days Mr. Plumley is expected to be charged with two additional murders, those of Karl and Melissa Brown.

In a statement delivered late this morning, she said, "We believe these deaths all to be connected. Mr. Plumley is a deranged individual. Under the delusion that he was protecting Ms. Johnson, he slaughtered her and everyone close to her. We can only be thankful that we apprehended him when we did, before he could cause any more mayhem."

When asked if these murders were related to the death of La Follette High School hockey star Ricky Piekowski, Detective Russell said, "We have evidence indicating that the late Karl Brown was responsible for [Mr. Piekowski's] death. What we now think is that in his obsessive fixation on Britney Johnson, Plumley believed that she had been the true target of that murder, and this spurred on his paranoid fantasies and eventually led him to carry out the murders."

thirty-eight

The clattering of wheels on iron, the constant clickety-click in his ears, the sway and bounce of the train as it made its way eastward, these things all made it difficult for Adam to doze off, despite the fact that his father had sprung for a sleeper compartment.

He lay awake for a long time, his hands locked behind his head, watching the shadows change shape as the reflection of the lights from outside roamed across the pebbled ceiling.

He was glad to be getting away.

And even though he dreaded returning to New Hampshire, he dreaded what might have happened if he'd stayed in Madison more.

On his last evening, he had worked up the courage to enter Britney's bedroom and collect the things he'd left there on that horrible morning. His socks, curled up in balls underneath the sheet. The underwear that Detective Russell had taunted him with.

He'd picked through the blankets piled sloppily next to the bed and, to make sure he hadn't missed anything, shook them out one at a time. As he flapped an old patchwork quilt, a small glint of metal had fallen to the floor, catching his eye.

It was a ring. Britney's diamond ring. He remembered her taking it off that night when they'd been together. She'd set it on the bedside table. It must have been knocked off and lost at some point during the night.

As he lay in his bunk unable to sleep, he studied it again. It was modest but beautiful.

What troubled him was that on the inner band, there was an engraving:

For Jan with All My Love—Ed 4/10/1985

Odd. It must have been Britney's mother's ring. She'd been lying about having received it from Ricky. Wishful thinking, figured Adam. She'd been so upset about her boyfriend's death that she'd invented a fantasy, a way to claim him forever.

Finally, when he managed to nod off, he had weird dreams.

He dreamed of Britney. The sense of her. The feeling that she was here with him.

He couldn't see her, but in his dream, he smelled the vanilla and cinnamon of her perfume. He heard her voice—not the pitched sarcasm of her when she was angry, but the sugary purring way that she had sounded on that night they'd spent cuddled together on her bed.

She was saying, "Should I do it?" and standing above a dark chasm—hundreds of thousands of miles deep.

"No," he responded. "Stay with me. The moon is down there and we want to stay in the sun."

"But it's dark here too," she said. "The better idea is if you jump with me."

"I don't want to, though."

He was sweating. He could see her clearly now.

She flipped the blond hair out of her face and smiled with her eyes.

His stomach spun over itself and he wanted to touch her.

"Let's do it tomorrow," he said. "Why don't you climb up here and curl up with me? Let's hold each other just this one last time."

Her smile crept slowly down from her eyes, spread over her whole face, cockeyed, wry, mischievous.

She moved so excruciatingly slowly. As if she were underwater. Her hair hung above her like it was alive. The color faded from it. It wasn't blond anymore; now it was black.

He opened his arms and embraced her.

Her body was warm next to his, soft, luscious. It felt so real that he couldn't believe he was dreaming. She didn't smell like perfume anymore; she smelled musty now.

She whispered in his ear, "Do you like that?"

"It's all I've ever wanted, Britney," he said.

She spun over him, straddled him. Her face had turned

hard. Her eyes were black. She was heavy on his chest. The pain he felt where her knee dug into his rib cage was real.

"Don't call me that," she said.

She was doing something with her hands behind her back. He couldn't see what, but suddenly, he was full of fear.

"Call me Jan."

"But you're Britney!"

"Haven't you heard? Britney's dead."

Her hands were above her head now. Something shimmered in them. It was too dark to tell what it was.

He wanted the dream to end now. It wasn't turning out the way he'd thought it would. He wanted to wake up, just for a moment, and start again at the point where the dream had turned ugly, to return it to sweetness and keep it there.

Then, with a shudder, he realized he *was* awake. The dream *had* ended and Britney really *was* here, straddling him.

It was too late.

The knife was already sliding into his chest. Blood was oozing out onto his T-shirt, running down onto the sheets below him and soaking through the mattress.

He was never going to wake up again.

thirty-nine

The sun was shining. The leaves on the trees rustled and swayed. The grass was a vibrant color of green. Cute boys in knee-length shorts were playing hacky sack. It was a beautiful day and Britney was free, far away in Ithaca, New York.

She smiled. She'd dyed her hair jet black and straightened it, cutting the bangs. She was a whole new person.

When she waved at the cutest of the cute boys, the one with the stringy shoulder-length hair, he nodded at her, his eyes twinkling. After the game broke up, he introduced himself. Nick. He was a freshman at Cornell.

She told him her name was Jan.

They talked for a while, then he invited her up to hang out in his dorm room, and she thought he was so cute she couldn't say no.

"Where are you from?" he said, leaning back on his bed. He was shirtless and tan. "Ithaca's a pretty small town. I figure I would have seen you around before."

She was sitting on top of his blond wood desk, and she leaned in toward him. "Can you keep a secret?" she asked.

When he nodded, she went on. "You're never going to believe this, but I'm running for my life."

Given all she'd accomplished so far, she felt like she could do anything now.

She told him the whole story.

"I know this girl named Britney who killed her mother a few years ago—don't get me wrong, her mother was crazy. She'd been tormenting her for her entire life. And one day she just couldn't take it anymore. Their family went on a rafting trip, and she and her boyfriend Karl drowned her."

"Jesus!" Nick said.

"Everyone thought it was an accident, and that would have been the end of it, but when Karl went to jail on a drug charge, she started dating this jock guy named Ricky.

"If only Ricky had loved her less. If only he hadn't tried so hard to find the answers to her mother's death. He should have left things as they were. He should have believed her when she said she didn't want to know. Then everything would have been fine. But he had to go snooping. He had to follow his suspicions—even though they were leading him toward discovering the horrible secret she'd hidden from him.

"She had to do something before she got caught. Karl was

still in love with her, and once he got out of jail, she convinced him to kill Ricky."

Britney felt like she was falling into a trance, as though the events she was relating had happened to someone else, not her.

She reached over and took Nick's hand, gazed at his delicate knuckles for a moment before kissing the base of his thumb and letting his hand go again.

"After that, things started to unravel. Karl became insanely jealous. She told him it was over between them, but he wouldn't take no for an answer. She had to kill him. And then she was off, killing any and everyone who came anywhere near discovering the truth about what she'd been doing.

"Since I knew the whole truth about her, she especially wanted to get to me. I barely escaped. We were on a lake, frozen over for the winter, but the weather had turned and the ice was thin. I fell in—or more likely, she pushed me in; we were tussling and it was hard to tell which.

"I had to swim for my life, blindly, following my instincts, heading off randomly, hoping against hope that I would find an opening before I ran out of air. It was terrifying. I still can't believe I made it. I took off running and I haven't stopped since."

She gauged Nick's response. He was speechless. His eyes were popping out of his head.

"I'm really lucky to have gotten away," she said.

"That's just . . ." he said. "That's out of control!"

"That's the thing about this girl, though," said Britney. "She was completely controlled. She almost never made a mistake.

I can only think of one." She remembered Adam and twisted the ring on her finger.

"What was it?"

Her eyes darted around the room like she was looking for someone in the shadows.

"I can't tell you that."

"Why not?"

"She might find out."

The muscles in his neck and shoulders tensed briefly. He was starting to get spooked.

"How would she know?"

"Oh, she'd know. She has a way of finding these things out."

He jumped from the bed and threw a T-shirt on. "Let's go," he said. "We should tell the police about this."

Britney shouted, "No!" Then turning sweet again, she said, "Why would I want to do that?"

"I don't know why you haven't gone to them already. . . . I mean, if this girl's still at large—"

The color drained from his face as the truth sank in.

She cocked her head and smiled an ambiguous smile. Her hand trailed up toward an area just above her heart and she ran her finger over the spot where she used to toy with the hockey pin on Ricky's letter jacket. She wondered if Nick could guess what she was planning to do next.